RICHARD L. B

MURDER
IN TIP-UP TOWN

[A COLD CASE]

OTHER BOOKS
BY RICHARD L. BALDWIN

FICTION:

A Lesson Plan for Murder (1998)
ISBN: 0-9660685-0-5. Buttonwood Press.

The Principal Cause of Death (1999)
ISBN: 0-9660685-2-1. Buttonwood Press.

Administration Can Be Murder (2000)
ISBN: 0-9660685-4-8. Buttonwood Press.

Buried Secrets of Bois Blanc: Murder in the Straits of Mackinac (2001)
ISBN: 0-9660685-5-6. Buttonwood Press.

The Marina Murders (2003)
ISBN: 0-9660685-7-2. Buttonwood Press.

A Final Crossing: Murder on the S.S. Badger (2004)
ISBN: 0-9742920-2-8. Buttonwood Press.

Poaching Man and Beast: Murder in the North Woods (2006)
ISBN: 0-9742920-3-6. Buttonwood Press.

The Lighthouse Murders (2007)
ISBN: 978-0-9742920-5-2. Buttonwood Press.

Murder in Thin Air (2008)
ISBN: 978-0-9742920-9-0. Buttonwood Press.

Murder at the Ingham County Fair (2009)
ISBN: 978-0-9823351-0-9. Buttonwood Press.

The Searing Mysteries: Three in One (2001)
ISBN: 0-9660685-6-4. Buttonwood Press.

The Moon Beach Mysteries (2003)
ISBN: 0-9660685-9-9. Buttonwood Press.

The Detective Company (2004; written with Sandie Jones.)
ISBN: 0-9742920-0-1. Buttonwood Press.

SPIRITUAL:

Unity and the Children (2000)
ISBN: 0-9660685-3-X. Buttonwood Press.

NON-FICTION:

The Piano Recital (1999)
ISBN: 0-9660685-1-3. Buttonwood Press.

A Story to Tell: Special Education in Michigan's Upper Peninsula 1902-1975 (1994)
ISBN: 932212-77-8. Lake Superior Press.

Warriors and Special Olympics: The Wertz Warrior Story (2006)
ISBN: 0-9742920-4-4. Buttonwood Press, LLC.

This novel is a product of the imagination of the author. None of the events described in this story occurred. No characters in the story are intended to portray by description, personality, or behaviors those associated currently or in the past with the actual Tip-Up Town festival. Though settings, buildings, and businesses may exist, liberties may have been taken as to actual locations and descriptions. This story has no purpose other than to entertain the reader.

Published by Buttonwood Press
P.O. Box 716
Haslett, Michigan 48840
www.buttonwoodpress.com

ISBN: 978-0-9823351-2-3
Printed in the United States of America

2010
Dedication

I dedicate this book to my friend, Jack Kelly, who died on Monday, November 16, 2009. He loved my stories. With his permission, I first introduced Jack as Lou's cohort in "The Lighthouse Murders," published in 2006. His welcome advice regarding subsequent drafts was right on. I shall miss Jack, but he will live on in my stories as long as I am able to write them.

Thanks my friend, and rest in peace.

ACKNOWLEDGEMENTS

Thank you to my editor, Anne Ordiway; proofreader, Joyce Wagner; graphic designer, Sarah Thomas; and my director of marketing, Martha Rooker.

I also thank the following people for their cooperation and assistance in the telling of this story: Joe Hoffmeister, Jack Kelly, Richard and Paula Doucette, B.J. Morrison, Jerry Weiss, Jim Meyers, Bob Gillespie, Ben Strasz, Tim Strasz, Tim Foster, Steven Dunckel, and Lisa Stearns.

The cover photo of fishing shanties on Houghton Lake was taken by Michael Drouillard of Druid Oaks Photography. The photos on pages 33–34 were taken by Adam Janke.

Last but not least, I thank Patty Baldwin, whose love and support bring me much joy.

TIP-UP TOWN, USA

In 1950, two Houghton Lake characters, Bob Carman and Bob Sweet, came up with the idea of a winter festival as a way to have some fun while increasing tourism in the Houghton Lake area. The festival gets its name from a "tip-up," a short colorful device used to alert the fisherman to a bite. When the fish takes the bait, the fishing line which is connected to a spring mechanism, pops up indicating action below the ice.

Tip-Up Town boasts a mayor, a beauty queen, and a host of contests for all ages. Any contest you might imagine has probably been held during the last 60 years. In addition, participants can enjoy a parade, carnival rides, fishing contests, snowmobile races, a Polar Bear Dip, and an on-the-ice softball game. The festival offers something for everyone and families return year after year to shake off mid-winter cabin fever.

Each year commemorative buttons are sold and a prize winner is selected. During my research for this novel, I met Kim Kurtz who in 1995 won a snowmobile, the Grand Prize. Congratulations, Kim!

For more information on Tip-Up Town, go to www.tip-up-townusa.com and please plan to attend the 61st offering of fun and tomfoolery in January of 2011.

CHAPTER
ONE

Lou Searing watched the 6:00 WOOD News, an NBC affiliate in Grand Rapids. As a major winter storm approached the west Michigan shoreline, more than twenty inches were predicted by morning and snow was expected during most, if not all, of the next day. Lou called to Carol, his wife, from the living room of their two-story house on the shore of Lake Michigan.

"You might want to see this weather report. We're liable to be hit pretty hard."

"That's all I've heard about today," Carol replied, coming into the living room. She threw up her hands in exasperation as she added, "You'd think the Ice Age were returning. This is Michigan—it's winter. Why is this news?"

"It's just that this storm is expected to be big, is all," Lou replied.

"I was at the grocery store this afternoon, along with hundreds of stock-piling Grand Havenites. I've never seen so many empty shelves in my life," Carol continued, still not in a good mood.

"Just taking precautions, would be my guess," Lou replied.

"I understand, but snow falls, schools close, meetings are cancelled, snow plow companies smile all the way to the bank. And in a day or two, we're all back to normal. It's the Michigan winter way of life."

"Do we have the makings of hot chocolate?" Lou asked, trying to change the subject.

"You're lucky there. I got the last containers of chocolate mix and coffee cream."

"Hot chocolate can get me through anything."

"I've questions for you: is the generator ready to go?" Carol asked. "Do you have gas for the snowblower? Do we have dog and cat food for Samm and Millie?"

"Check, check, and check. I say, bring on the snow," Lou replied.

"And I'll bring on the hot chocolate," Carol replied smiling, apparently over her frustration with talk of the "storm of the decade."

"A fire in the fireplace, one of your hand-crafted afghans over my knees, hot chocolate in my hand, you beside me, and the Red Wings on TV. Sounds like heaven to me," Lou said with contentment.

"It would be heaven for me too, if you could replace the Red Wings with 'Heroes.'"

"Touché," Lou replied with a smile.

"I'll get the water on for hot chocolate." As Carol passed the front door, there was a loud rap on it. With a concerned expression, Carol looked at Lou as he got out of his chair.

"Probably Vern from next door—wants to be sure I have an extra shovel," Lou said, walking to the door. "Happens every time we have snow."

Lou opened the door to find a man and a woman who appeared to be in their forties and were dressed as if they were going to a formal event.

"Can I help you?" Lou asked, surprised that anyone would be out on this stormy eve.

The man nodded. "Mr. Searing?"

"Yes."

"I'm Todd Moody and this is Mary Jones," the visitor said, extending his hand in greeting. "May we speak with you for a few minutes?"

"I suppose. Come in. This is my wife Carol." The three smiled and nodded as the visitors entered, stomping snow from their boots. "I sure hope you folks are local. It's not a night to be travelling. There's a winter storm brewing."

"We're from St. Helen—I'm guessing you don't know where that is," Mary smiled.

Lou closed the door firmly. "Let me take your coats. And I do know of St. Helen," Lou replied, proud of his knowledge of Michigan geography. "I spoke at the community center there a couple of years ago—even ate dinner at the Peach Pit. St. Helen was the boyhood home of Charlton Heston. And, it holds an annual bluegill festival," Lou continued, impressing his guests with his knowledge of their community.

"Do you work for the Chamber of Commerce?" Todd asked.

"No, I gave a talk there about writing mysteries, and I met a lot of wonderful people!"

Carol went into the kitchen to make sure water was boiling for two more cups of cocoa, while Lou hung up the heavy coats in the front closet. As he placed Todd's hat on the upper shelf he asked, "What brings you to our front door on the eve of a major winter storm?"

"We're in town for a wedding at the Presbyterian Church," Mary replied. "At the reception we were talking to a couple of your neighbors who told us of your detective work."

"Probably Dick and Janice," Lou surmised. "They said they were going to a wedding this weekend. Come into the living room and have a seat."

"Yes, Dick and Janice. Anyway, the topic of 'cold cases' came up, because Janice was talking about a recent TV show concerning a case solved some forty years after the crime occurred." Carol came into the living room and sat on the sofa next to Lou.

"Not to rush to the reason for your visit, but it's sounding like there's a cold case you want me to solve," Lou remarked, thinking that the Red Wings game was under way, and he was missing the action.

"Exactly," Todd replied. "Janice said you usually investigate murders soon after they're committed. I explained the cold case, and Dick thought it wouldn't hurt to mention it to you. If you have some spare time, maybe you would take it on."

"I'm not working on a case at the moment, but I'd have to know more about the situation before I could commit myself," Lou replied, wanting to leave room to reject the request. "Perhaps we could talk about it sometime."

"Is now inconvenient?" Mary asked, as Carol went to pour water for hot cocoa. This would not be a five-minute visit.

"Are you sure you shouldn't get going ahead of this storm? Or do you have a reservation at a motel?" Lou asked. He was more interested in seeing the Red Wings game than worrying about his guests being stranded in the storm.

"You don't know Todd, and you probably didn't notice the Hummer in your drive," Mary said, smiling. "Todd *lives* for these storms. He likes the challenge."

"Well, then tell me about this cold case—pun intended," Lou said, returning her smile. Carol entered the living room carrying a tray with four cups of hot chocolate and a plate of warm chocolate chip cookies.

"Are you a quilter, Mrs. Searing?" Mary asked, admiring a quilt folded on the back of a wingback chair.

"Oh, yes. I love to quilt," Carol replied, happy that someone asked about her passion. "I suppose I enjoy quilting as much as Lou enjoys solving a murder. Would you like to see my quilting room, or would you rather stay here?" Carol asked Mary.

"I would much rather talk quilting and see your studio," Mary replied.

"Okay, let's go upstairs and talk fat quarters and applique and leave the cold case details to the men." Mary and Carol rose, carrying cups of cocoa, napkins, and cookies up the stairs.

Lou and Todd also helped themselves to the refreshments, settling in for a talk.

"Before we begin, would you mind if I have the Red Wings game on TV with the sound muted?" Lou asked. "I'm a fan, and I'd like to check the score from time to time, and maybe see the replays. My lack of manners is showing, I guess."

"On the contrary, I'm interested in the game myself, but talking with you is a much higher priority for me."

"I understand," Lou said as he picked up the remote, found ESPN, and muted the sound. He noted that the game was still scoreless after a few minutes of play.

Blowing the steam off his cup of cocoa, Lou settled into his leather chair and trained his left eye on the Red Wings and his right eye on Todd. "Okay, I guess we're set. Tell me about your unsolved case."

"Actually, there's not a lot to tell," Todd began. "The missing person is my grandfather, Harry Moody. At the time of his disappearance, he lived with my grandmother in Houghton Lake and he was fifty-two years old. I was sixteen then—I'm forty-two now—and I remember going fishing with 'Gramps,' as I called him. I remember him as a rugged outdoorsman. Growing up, I heard stories of Gramps that, quite frankly, could be fact, legend, or something in the middle."

"So all you know is that your grandfather disappeared? Was he killed or did he get tired of the cold and just leave town for warmer climes?" Lou asked.

"All we know is that he disappeared. His wallet was found in some woods near Houghton Lake with his ID and money in it. Nobody has ever found his body or any other personal item."

"If he was killed, the killer probably tossed the wallet into the woods to give the impression your grandfather had been there instead of where he really was," Lou reasoned.

"That makes sense," Todd replied.

"Did the local newspaper report on his disappearance?" Lou asked.

"I saw a couple of clippings in the Moody family Bible within the last several years. Grandma Moody kept them there, because her daily prayer was that Gramps would just walk in the front door."

"Which newspaper?" Lou asked.

"I don't know the exact name, but it would have to have been whatever newspaper published in the Houghton Lake area."

"Okay, I'll research it. Do you have a date for your Gramps' disappearance?" Lou asked.

"It was winter, but I don't recall a month or the day. If you'll research it, does this mean you're taking the case?" Todd asked.

"I suppose it does," Lou admitted. "I'm at loose ends at the moment, and Carol will be relieved to know that I'm not in the crosshairs of some trigger-happy character who doesn't exactly appreciate my snooping. Right?"

"I guess so," Todd replied. "What is your fee, Mr. Searing?"

"I don't have a fee as such, but I'll ask you to pay mileage for any traveling I do. Also, I would like the rights to your story, because I write a book about each case I solve."

"As far as rights go, absolutely."

"I have a simple contract for you to sign," Lou said, making a mental note to follow through.

"I'd be glad to. I simply want to know what happened to Gramps. Not knowing what happened to his father tormented my dad. I promised Dad on his deathbed that I would do what I could to find out what had happened to Gramps."

"Even if it is morbid, sad, and not a positive outcome?" Lou asked, alerting Todd to gruesome possibilities.

"After so many years, our imaginations have conjured up all kinds of disasters. So, peace would come with knowing whatever really happened."

"I understand," Lou said. "You said your dad has passed. Is your mother living?"

"Yes. Her name is Sherri," Todd replied. "She lives in Prudenville, near Houghton Lake. She keeps to herself."

"I think I can take this on," Lou said, wondering if he should think more before making the commitment.

"Thanks so much, Mr. Searing," Todd said, extending his hand. "Now, I suppose we should try to out-run this storm. Mary made it sound like 'the worse the better,' but I'm not as brave as she implied."

"Maturity checks some of youth's enthusiasm," Lou replied.

The two men glanced at the TV and saw the score was 1-1. "You haven't missed much, Lou. Besides, they'll replay the scoring. That's what's nice about television coverage—you get to see the exciting action over and over."

"I look forward to these games all day, only to find myself falling asleep by the end of the first period," Lou admitted.

Carol and Mary came downstairs discussing colors and patterns. "What a marvelous quilting studio!" Mary exclaimed. "If you need to come up with a Christmas present for me, Todd, you could replicate Carol's quilting room."

"I'll get your coats," Lou said, hoping to spare Todd the specifics of Carol's crafting playground.

"You can tell me all about it on our way home," Todd said, following Lou to the closet. The couples exchanged handshakes as Todd and Mary donned their coats. Lou opened the door to a blur of snow. Several inches had already fallen, and the wind was creating small eddies of snow here and there.

"It's nasty," Carol said, shivering as she viewed the scene.

"Todd loves it," Mary said, patting Todd on the shoulder. Todd caught Lou's eye and shook his head back and forth, slightly smiling.

"We'll be in touch," Todd called as the couple trudged to their Hummer in the snow-covered driveway. "I have your card; I'll probably call in the next day or two, unless the electricity is out."

"Thanks for the cookies and cocoa, Mrs. Searing," Mary shouted. Carol nodded.

Lou closed the door. "We'd never head out into this, Lou!" Carol said firmly.

"You have that right," Lou admitted, heading upstairs.

"Hey, what happened to sitting next to me with the afghan, hot chocolate, and the Red Wings?" Carol asked.

"I want to start in on this cold case, and besides, you want to watch 'Heroes.'"

"Wait—here's a weather bulletin on TV. You don't want to miss this," Carol said.

The WOOD TV weatherman appeared on the screen, superimposed over radar images in the background.

> *This could be the storm of the decade. The State Police have closed US-31 from Muskegon to Holland. Snow is falling along the shoreline at the rate of two inches per hour, with 30 mile-per-hour winds causing significant drifting. As the storm moves east, State Police expect to close I-96 from Muskegon to Grand Rapids because county crews can't keep up with the heavy snow. On your screen is a list of churches offering shelter to stranded motorists. Stay tuned to WOOD TV for updates. Unless you have an emergency, please stay off the roads so plows and emergency vehicles can do their jobs.*

When regular programming returned, the Red Wings had scored a goal and were leading the St. Louis Blues, 2-1.

Todd and Mary were taking the most dangerous ride of their lives. The Hummer had no problem moving through the snow, but visibility was almost nil. If a driver wasn't familiar with the road, he really was driving blind. Street lights in cities and suburbs provided some direction, but outside the city limits travelers were basically at the mercy of their guardian angels— except for the occasional glimpse of a vehicle's red taillights twenty yards ahead.

❄❄❄❄❄

Up in his warm second-floor office, Lou switched on his computer, connected to the Internet, and typed "Houghton Lake, MI newspaper" into the search space. Within seconds, *The Houghton Lake Resorter* appeared on his screen. Lou typed "Harry Moody" into the "Archives" section of the web site. Three articles from 1985 appeared.

The first article, dated January 18, 1985, provided some basic information.

> *Harry Moody of Houghton Lake was reported missing after he didn't return home last evening. Because of the Tip-Up Town festivities, Mrs. Estelle Moody thought he was out late visiting bars and talking with friends. When he didn't call or come home by morning, and he wasn't found in his fishing shanty, she became concerned. Police are asking that anyone who saw Mr. Moody or talked with him yesterday contact the Houghton Lake Police Department.*

The second article, dated a week later, provided readers with an update.

Moody Still Missing

> *Police report that a wallet belonging to Harry Moody was found during a ground search of a wooded area just east of Houghton Lake, approximately five miles from the city limits. The wallet contained Moody's driver's license and credit cards, along with paper money. Mrs. Moody reports that she has had no contact with her husband since he left*

home the evening of January 17. Police are still hopeful that Mr. Moody will return or that additional items belonging to him will be found.

Carol shouted from the living room. "You're missing a good hockey game! The Red Wings are ahead three to one!"

"*You're* watching the *hockey* game?" Lou said, surprised by Carol's report.

"'Heroes' was a rerun, and nothing else seems interesting. Come on down—it's warm, and your Red Wings are playing their hearts out."

"I have one more article to read. Be right there."

The third article offered nothing new regarding Harry's whereabouts, but presented a new aspect that warranted further investigation. "*According to a friend, Harry told people in a bar that he expected to come into a lot of money.*"

Lou printed the three articles and turned off the computer. Sharing a televised hockey game with Carol would be a rare experience, and he didn't want to miss it.

Carol had drawn a fresh cup of cocoa for Lou along with one chocolate chip cookie. Millie, the cat, was enjoying the fireplace from the braided rug in front of it. So Lou entered heaven—time with Carol, a hockey game on his big screen TV, a chocolate chip cookie, and hot cocoa. With the snow swirling outside, he cherished the warmth.

When the Red Wings put it away in the third quarter, visibility was practically zero. Lou turned on the porch light, but saw nothing beyond the whirling snow. He took a shovel and cleared a spot for Samm, their golden retriever, to relieve herself before going to her bed. While food and fresh water for Millie went into bowls, the 11:00 television news began.

The major storm we predicted on our 6:00 newscast has materialized. The National Weather Service has recorded eight inches of snow since the storm began around 7:30. Snowmobilers from Grand Haven, Ferrysburg, and Spring Lake have been providing emergency food and medicine, and have been transporting stranded motorists to area churches that have opened their doors to travelers caught in this extensive storm. Normally we would have a live report from somewhere in our viewing area, but police have asked that no one use public roads until an "all clear" is issued. If you need emergency help, call 911, and a snowmobile club member or an emergency vehicle will come to you.

Just as Carol turned out the downstairs lights, the phone rang, sending a shot of adrenaline to Lou's stomach. The call had to be related to the weather, but the unknown aspect concerned Lou. He hoped it was a wrong number or a friend checking on how the Searings were handling the storm.

"I'll get it," Lou said as he reached for the phone. "Hello."

"Lou, this is Dick. I'm sorry to call at this hour, but I noticed your lights, so I knew you were up."

"Is it snowing at your place?" Lou asked, lighthearted with relief.

"Is snow in the forecast?" Dick asked going along with Lou's humor.

"What's on your mind, Dick?" Lou asked wanting to finish the call.

"Janice and I met a couple from somewhere in the mid-Michigan area at a late-afternoon reception. They were talking about a cold case involving a member of his family. I mentioned that you investigated crimes and suggested that they contact you. So, this is a 'heads up' that you might get a call from them."

"Too late. They stopped here after the reception," Lou replied. "They seemed a nice couple. Mr. Moody talked about his grandfather's disappearance 25-plus years ago."

"I had hoped to alert you before they contacted you."

"Alert?" Lou asked. "Why do you use that word?"

"Well, rumor has it that these people take every opportunity to get into people's homes. They use their visit to check out the homes with thoughts of returning and breaking in later."

"How do you know this?" Lou asked.

"Some friends of ours saw us conversing with the couple and after they left, the friends told us we should never allow the two into our home. Now I feel terrible for suggesting they talk with you."

"No problem. We can have our locks changed if necessary, and Samm is a pretty good watchdog, you know."

"I'm sorry, Lou."

"Nothing to be concerned about, Dick. Going to need my shovel tomorrow?"

"It'll take more than a shovel to dig us out of this one."

"The Weather Channel makes it sound like Mother Nature will take most of Lake Michigan, crystallize it, and dump it on shore," Lou replied. "A storm like this is to the Weather Channel like the Emmy Awards are to the major networks. Oh well, I suppose we've seen worse."

"And, we'll deal with it, as usual. Again, sorry for directing those people to you, Lou."

"All is well. Thanks for the call." Lou, who seldom kept anything from Carol, decided not to tell her what Dick had said. She just didn't need such a concern now, or at any other time, for that matter.

The Searings went to bed, thankful for a warm bed and each other. Outside, the wind rattled windows, snow continued to fall, and calls to 911 were frequent.

❄✳❄✳❄

JANUARY 10TH

Sunday morning's light allowed residents to pry open doors, begin moving snow, and let pets out. Snowblowers were fired up in order to shift drifts from walks and drives into areas that, just a short while before, had been green. Carol was up making coffee for Lou, tea for herself, and oatmeal for the both of them.

An amateur photographer, she wanted to get proof of all the snow to send to friends and relatives in the South and Midwest. She felt they should be thankful to live in temperate climates and not to have their lives disrupted by Mother Nature.

Lou was in no hurry to work at snow removal because he wouldn't be going out on the county road leading to a city street. Besides, he had learned after years of plowing the driveway that within an hour of completing his work, the county plow would fill up the apron of the drive with snow from the road. Lou would shout, "C'mon, can't we work together on this job?" The plow driver would wave and occasionally toot his horn.

Carol was anxious to get bird seed into the feeders, but getting to the feeders was out of the question. So, like a farmer throwing corn to his chickens, Carol threw handfuls of seed out onto the crusty snow. The birds who hadn't rolled over to catch a few more winks appreciated the feeding from their dependable friend.

Television reporters advised viewers of cancelled church services, suspended city and county services, and no Monday mail delivery. Citizens were asked to stay off the roads so crews could try to keep up with the falling snow. Radar images on the Weather Channel showed a continuous flow of frigid air coming west to east over Lake Michigan caused by an intense low pressure system centered over Wisconsin's Door Peninsula.

Lou and Carol enjoyed hot oatmeal and their coffee and tea.

"Looks like we'll have a day cooped up at home," Lou said.

"I'll call St. Pat's and see if they need any help with stranded folks," Carol decided. "I'm sure I can find a ride on the back of a snowmobile."

"That's mighty kind of you," Lou replied. "It doesn't surprise me. You're an angel."

"How will you spend the day?" Carol asked.

"I guess I'll look for more info about this cold case I took on last evening."

"I'm so thankful you'll finally be investigating something where no one wants to end your life."

"That isn't guaranteed, but whoever killed Harry Moody is most likely dead, or at least too old to be dangerous."

Carol bundled up for a blustery snowmobile ride to St. Pat's. Lou kissed her goodbye, hugged her, and told her, "I'm proud of you for helping others."

CHAPTER
TWO

Lou Searing was sixty-nine years young. He had hearing loss in both ears, but two over-the-ear hearing aids helped. He was overweight, but only comfortably so. And, he was past that time in life when Rogaine might be an option. At his age, he simply allowed his body to be itself, and if a love of chocolate and other sweets put pounds on a six-foot frame, so be it.

Carol Searing was beautiful, charming, and a delight to all who knew her. Her mission was service to others, whether in their church, at the Ronald McDonald House, or through her quilt groups. She loved Lou for a number of reasons and supported him in his interests, some of which seemed unsafe and unwise to her, like riding his Harley Davidson and searching for killers.

Lou and Carol had both enjoyed long careers in special education. Lou had been a teacher of children with hearing loss, serving as a public school teacher, university professor, and a state employee for twenty years in the Michigan Department of

Education. Carol had been a teacher in Kansas, and after several years of classroom teaching she earned a masters degree from the University of Kansas in teaching the deaf. She then taught children with hearing loss, supervised programs, and finished her career as an in-home teacher, serving parents and young children with disabilities.

Lou and Carol lived in a beautiful home in the dunes south of Grand Haven, Michigan. Lou had explained to the architect that he wanted a second-floor office, and Carol a second-floor quilting studio. As each followed his/her passion, they enjoyed views of Lake Michigan during every season of the year.

Rounding out the Searing family were their pets—Samm, a golden retriever who had lost the use of her right front leg after an injury several years before, and Millie, the cat, who allowed other family members to live in 'her' home, as long as they served her and met her every need.

One joy of living so close to the lake was walking along the shore during the warmer months. Not only did this activity provide exercise, but Lou and Carol, walking hand and hand, and sometimes pulling Samm in her Red Flyer wagon, could take time together to exchange thoughts and enjoy sunsets.

❄✳❄✳❄

Jack Kelly, a 62-year-old native of Muskegon, Michigan, had been Lou's assistant in investigating Michigan murders for several years. Jack's contribution to Lou's team was intelligence.

Jack had enjoyed a successful career as an accountant before retiring for health reasons. He was sharp as a tack, able to see the big picture, and paid a lot of attention to detail which was an important contrast to Lou.

Lou called Jack to tell him about Harry Moody. "Bet you're snowed in?"

"Yes. We got it as bad as you did, Lou."

"Carol headed off on the back of a snowmobile to help at church. I guess they were very glad she called."

"Elaine is doing what she loves to do," Jack explained.

"Let me guess," Lou interrupted. "She's riding your John Deere lawn mower snowplow combination and moving snow from here to there."

"Exactly."

"Well, good for her! And, you're watching Regis and Kelly?" Lou asked.

"No, that's not for me. I'm wrapping pipes in the basement to keep water flowing into our house."

"That's right, you have a history of trouble with frozen pipes."

"Why do I get the feeling you didn't call me just to find out how I'm spending the morning?"

"I accepted a case last evening, and I want to tell you about it, in hopes you'll work with me on it."

"You know my answer is yes. Every time the phone rings, Elaine knows I'm hoping it's you inviting me into your next case. So, what's up? I haven't heard anything big in the news the last few days."

"It's a cold case, Jack."

"Pun intended? Or is it really a *cold* case?"

"It's really a cold case," Lou replied. "A man disappeared during the Tip-Up Town Ice Fishing Festival in Houghton Lake about 25 years ago. His grandson stopped by last night to ask me to look into it."

"The guy drove over in this storm?"

"He and a friend were in town for a wedding, and at the reception he talked to a neighbor of mine who told him about my investigations. So, being in town, they came to talk to me."

"I see. Was the guy murdered?" Jack asked.

"Don't know. His body was never found—he could have simply skipped town, or he may have even been kidnapped. I checked the local newspaper archives on line last evening and read that he was reported missing during the 1985 ice-fishing festival. His wallet was later found in a wooded area near Houghton Lake. But, the local paper, The Resorter, noted that he had told a friend he was coming into a lot of money."

"This doesn't sound easy. Not that any of them are, Lou. What else did you learn?" Jack asked.

"That's it; you now know what I know. We're standing at the starting line."

"Just tell me what you want me to do, and I'll be right on it. You know that," Jack said. "Remember, Lou, I'm to you as Sancho was to Don Quixote—the faithful servant."

"I appreciate that. First of all, nothing will happen until we can drive over to Houghton Lake. Then we'll talk to people who knew this guy. By the way, the man's name is Harry Moody."

"Okay, so you're just giving me a 'heads up.' Let me know when you can get out of your driveway."

"I'll talk with you soon, Jack. I hope you and your pipes remain thawed."

❄❄❄❄❄

In advance of their trip, Lou called the Houghton Lake librarian, Susan Abraham, and explained what he hoped to find. He also called the Houghton Lake Police Chief, Warren Lincoln, asking whether he could talk with the officers who had worked the Moody case in 1985. One detective had retired to Florida, but the other, Arthur Lockwood, was still on the force and would share what he could recall.

Three days after the storm, most of the roads in Grand Haven and in Ottawa County were clear, schools were open, and mail was being delivered. And, Jack could drive to Grand Haven.

On the way to Houghton Lake the morning of January 13, the farther Lou and Jack drove east, the less snow had fallen.

Houghton Lake was probably the closest thing to a year-round outdoorsman's paradise as one could find. Two area lakes, Houghton and Higgins, provided opportunities for year-round fishing, and snowy winters offered snowmobiling, cross-country skiing, hiking, and a myriad of other cold-weather sports.

Around 10 a.m, Lou and Jack checked into the Holiday Inn Express. Not knowing how long they would be in town, they would reserve their rooms one night at a time. Once assured of a place to sleep, the two headed for the library.

Librarian Susan Abraham, who had been expecting them, provided Lou and Jack with a bulging reference folder including newspaper articles, a Tip-Up Town Festival program for 1985, and even a series of photos from the 1985 festival. Finally, she presented them with a list she had compiled of residents still in the area who might remember Harold Moody.

After thanking Susan for her help, the two headed to the police station to interview Art Lockwood, the police officer who had been working for the Houghton Lake police in 1985. After introductions, handshakes were exchanged.

Lou began. "My guess is you're the person who knows the most about Harry Moody's case."

"Well, it was a long time ago, but the file contents jogged my memory. We usually get our man, Lou. In a town this small, everyone knows everyone else. It's generally easy to come up with a witness or two and gather reliable evidence; an arrest usually follows an interrogation—but this case didn't work out that way."

"Why was that?" Lou asked.

"It was a classic example of what we didn't have and what we didn't find," Sergeant Detective Lockwood replied.

"Meaning?"

"Meaning, we didn't find a body, a weapon, a motive, any witnesses. Moody simply dropped off the face of the earth. We found his wallet in the woods, but that's it. Friends who were the last to see him were no help. One said Moody told him that he was coming into a lot of money. Another said he was going south to get warm, even if he had to live a bum's life. It seemed like whenever we got a lead, we found a contradictory indication."

"Was his family any help?" Jack asked.

"Oh yes, Mrs. Moody was very helpful. Her name is Estelle; she still lives in their home here in Houghton Lake. As I said, Harry simply disappeared. Either he moved on, or someone pulled off the perfect murder. We didn't have forensic evidence-gathering skills at the time, and we found no fingerprints on the wallet except Harry's. We put out several 'Be On the Lookout' bulletins, but we never got a call. We worked on it for a good year, but by then, we had nothing to ask people, and we had no new information. We preserved the case, letting Mrs. Moody know that we would resume work on it if we had another lead."

Lou turned to Jack. "Maybe I bit off more than I can chew this time." Jack simply nodded, indicating he had nothing to add.

"What can you tell me about Moody's grandson, Todd? I think he lives in this area."

"Todd Moody. You know him?" Sergeant Lockwood asked.

"I can't say that I 'know' him, but I've talked with him. He asked me to find out what happened to his grandfather."

"Since he's Harry's grandson, my guess is that Todd wants Harry's disappearance explained because he thinks he might gain a lot of cash if there is an insurance settlement, or if his grandfather's money can be found. You need to be careful with this guy, Lou. Folks around here think he has mental problems. Did he seem normal when you talked with him?"

"Other than his venturing out into a major snow storm, yes, I guess he seemed normal," Lou replied. "What challenges his mental health?"

"Rumor in the bar, is all, Lou, but you know there's often a kernel of truth in a rumor."

"Can you give me a list of people currently living in the area who knew Harry? I'd like to interview them. Susan Abraham at the library gave me a list, but the more possibilities the better my chances are of getting some information."

"I can do that. And, I offer my help with your work, if you need it. I can grease the skids, so you can get to the people you need to see."

"That's great. We'll call if we have questions or need your help. I would like a copy of the reports on Harry's disappearance and anything else in your files that might prove helpful."

"Sure. I'll dig them out of storage."

❄❄❄❄❄

Lou and Jack decided to visit the Northshore Lounge, where Harry was last seen. The two sat at a small table in the center of the room. It was late afternoon and they were both hungry. The waitress—Alice, according to her name tag—approached to take their order.

"I'll have your wet burrito and a Diet Coke," Lou told Alice, who nodded and wrote on her order pad.

"I think I'll get some rabbit food," Jack said. "Give me your small chef's salad with black coffee. And, if you've a cup of bean soup, I'd like that, too."

"Anything else?" Alice asked.

"Yes; is the owner here today?" Lou asked.

"He is. You want to talk to him?"

"Yes, please."

"I'll tell him." As Alice walked away, Lou glanced at the bartender, a bearded man who appeared to be about fifty.

Lou turned to Jack, "The odds are a million to one, but do you suppose that bartender was working here twenty-five years ago?"

"Stranger things have happened," Jack responded, rising to look at the photos covering the walls of the bar. Most of the photographs were of fish-catches, racks of deer, patrons of the bar, and events from past Tip-Up Town Ice Fishing Festivals. While Jack was looking at the photos, the owner came up to the table and shook Lou's hand.

"Alice said you wanted to see me. I'm Chuck MacKenzie. How can I help you?"

"I'm Lou Searing, and the gentleman over there is Jack Kelly. We're looking into the disappearance of Harry Moody, about 25 years ago."

"I remember that," Chuck replied.

"Did you own this bar then, Chuck?"

"My dad did, but I was his second-in-command until a few years ago when he signed it over to me."

"I see. Did you know Harry Moody?" Lou asked.

"We weren't friends, but I knew him. He pretty much stuck to his group of friends."

"Are those friends still living, and if so, can you give me names and addresses?"

Jack returned to the table, shook hands with Chuck, sat down, and began sipping his hot coffee.

"I only know two of his friends who are still living in town." Chuck called to Alice, asking her to bring him the phone book. Chuck thumbed through the book to the "S" section, moved his index finger down a column and stopped at an entry. "Here it is—Donny Stewart." Lou wrote down the name, phone number and address.

Chuck continued to thumb through the book. "Another of Harry's friends was Abbott Brick. His nickname is 'Buck,' and he actually answers only to Buck Brick." Lou noted the name, address, and phone number as Alice brought food to the table.

"Anything else you need from me?" Chuck asked

"Do you know Todd Moody?" Lou asked.

"I'm afraid I do," Chuck replied.

"And that means?" Lou asked.

"Let's just say, most kids on the playground know the bully. They don't like him, but they know him, and they try to stay clear of him."

"Why would you want to stay clear of Todd Moody?"

"For a lot of reasons I'd really prefer not to get into, if you don't mind."

"Do you remember anything after Harry's last visit to your bar?"

"Oh, yeah. His disappearance was big news in a small town. It put a damper on the Tip-Up Town Festival that year."

"What was it like?" Jack asked.

"I remember mixed reactions," Chuck began. "Some guys were vengeful, ready to get a posse together and find whoever killed Harry. Others thought the guy had it coming to him and everyone should let sleeping dogs lie. Harry was a 'love him or hate him' kind of guy.

"I remember Estelle Moody coming in here a couple of days later to thank people for helping to look for Harry. She was distraught over the whole mess. The festival folks were quite upset that their events were playing second fiddle to rumors that a resident had been killed. I also remember all sorts of theories, everything from: 'He just wanted to go to Florida, so he did,' to 'He was brutally murdered by someone who knew him.' That's about it."

"Thanks, Chuck," Lou said. "Here's my card in case you think of something else." Chuck took the card and said, "I'm glad you're on the case. Your investigation will revive interest in solving this once and for all."

When Chuck had left, Jack said, "You should look at the pictures on the wall, Lou. There's a lot of history up there, and if those walls could talk, we'd hear a lot of tall tales."

Lou asked Alice for a refill of his Diet Coke, and when she brought it, he asked, "Are any of the photos on your wall of Harry Moody?"

"Yeah, he's in some of them."

"Could you show me?" Lou asked, rising and following Alice to the array of photos. Jack joined them.

Alice pointed to one photo. "Here he is with his fishing buddies. In the dark of night, these four would come in and brag about the number and size of the bluegills they caught in their shanties."

"Do you know their names?" Lou asked.

"First of all, this is a rare photo. This picture was taken at a family wedding and the guys look fairly normal. They actually look like they bathed, brushed their hair, trimmed their beards. You might not recognize them if they walked into our bar on a regular day. They were pretty rugged guys. Anyway, the one on the left is Don Stewart, then Harry, then Buck Brick, and the one on the far right is George Zink."

"Who is this boy with Harry?" Lou asked, pointing to a slightly blurry photo on the wall.

"That's Todd Moody when he was a teenager. It was taken at that same family wedding."

"George Zink is no longer in the area, correct?"

"As far as I know."

"Is he living?" Lou asked.

"I don't know," Alice replied.

"Does he have any relatives here?" Jack asked.

"I think so, but I can't help you with that," Alice replied.

"That's quite a string of fish," Lou said, pointing to another photo on the wall.

"Yes, when they're biting, you can't beat ice fishing on Houghton Lake."

"I take it this is also Harry?" Lou asked, pointing to a photo of a bearded man and a young man with a rifle and a deer rack.

"Yes, it is. The date on the back is before November 15th, so Harry poached this one. Said he just couldn't wait another week."

"Who is that next to Harry?"

"That's Todd, his grandson."

"Really? Todd must have had a growth spurt. He lives in St. Helen now, right?" Lou asked.

"He lives around here, but I don't know where exactly."

"Is Todd's father still living?" Jack asked.

"No, he died a few years ago. He was named after Harry, but everyone called him 'Junior,' to keep them straight.

"Junior was against hunting—saw no sense in killing God's creatures—so Harry taught Todd how to hunt. He took the kid under his wing and vowed to 'make him a man.' Junior Moody never got over Harry saying that. In fact, some rumors had Junior responsible for killing his dad."

"Was Junior cleared in the case?" Lou asked.

"You'd have to ask the police."

"Thanks, Alice," Lou said, as he turned and headed back to the table.

After paying their bill and leaving Alice a hefty tip, Lou and Jack decided to call it a day. They'd had a long trip to Houghton Lake and talked with several people, so they returned to the motel to take a rest before dinner. Lou called Carol to see how she was doing, and Jack called Elaine to be assured all was well on the home front. Because of their late lunch, they enjoyed trips to the salad bar. Lou thought he might come back down for dessert later.

Before going to bed, Lou went to the bar, ordered some vanilla ice cream with chocolate sauce, and watched the hockey game between the Red Wings and the Chicago Black Hawks. He had been watching in his room, but he moved to the bar to take advantage of the big screen.

With a Red Wings victory assured and the dessert bowl empty, Lou left a tip on the table and ambled off to his room to get some sleep.

JANUARY 14

The next morning Lou and Jack met in the hotel lounge for a continental breakfast. "Sleep well, Jack?"

"Can't say I did, but then again, I seldom do," Jack replied. "How about you?"

"Don't think I slept for much more than an hour, thinking about this case. Hand me that *USA Today,* please."

"So, what did your thinking about the case tell you?" Jack asked, handing the paper to Lou.

"I want to go to the Tip-Up Town Festival office. I have a feeling that we'll find something interesting there."

❄❄❄❄❄

At the Festival office, Lou introduced himself and Jack to the director, Lois Wiggins, and explained the purpose of their mission. "We'd appreciate your help. You must be busy with this year's festival, so we'll try not to take much of your time and to stay out of the way."

"This Moody case has been a sore spot in the community for far too long. If we can help bring closure to it, all the better," Lois replied.

"Thank you. Basically, we're interested in your 1985 festival. We'd like to see any photos you have, and, if anyone on your staff worked the '85 festival, we'd like to talk to him or her."

"We have a file for each year of the festival, so that's easy enough. And a local family, the Bishops, are aerial photographers. They're known for spectacular photos of Houghton Lake during Tip-Up Town—hundreds of fish shanties are on the ice then. You're welcome to see photos from any year. Also, no one currently on staff worked the 1985 festival.

"I imagine you had a large network of volunteers," Lou said.

"Yes, I did. The leader of our 1985 volunteer corps, Traci Mueller, is still in the area. I can't imagine she would know anything helpful, but you asked for staff here in '85."

Lou jotted down Traci's name and continued his questions. "Did Harry have a shanty on Houghton Lake?"

"You'll have to ask his friends about that."

"If Jack and I can see your 1985 file with the aerial photos, we'll get to work."

"I'll be right back with those items. You can work in our conference room. We have a planning committee meeting this afternoon, but you're welcome to use the room this morning."

"You've been very helpful. Thanks."

❄❄❄❄❄

Lou and Jack spent the balance of the morning looking over the items in the festival's 1985 Festival folder, but nothing proved particularly useful. The Bishop family's aerial photos of the lake and its shanties were excellent, but at this point in the investigation, it was enough to know that the photos existed.

Next, Lou called Harry Moody's friends who were still in the area. Donny Stewart wanted nothing to do with someone who was poking around in his friend's disappearance, but Buck Brick was most willing to talk. He would meet them at Booners Restaurant.

Buck was a short man with a beard and moustache, who appeared to be in his early fifties. He seemed a bit more refined than Harry or Donny.

After introductions and small talk, Lou, Jack, and Buck placed their lunch orders. Once their drinks had arrived, Lou broached the subject. "Do you mind my calling you, Buck?"

"It's what everybody calls me. I wouldn't answer if someone called me anything else."

"Okay, thanks. As you know, Jack and I hope to explain Harry Moody's disappearance. As Harry's good friend, we're hoping you might be able to point us in the right direction."

"And, if you have a theory about what happened to him, we'd like to hear that as well," Jack added.

"I can do both," Buck replied. "You just want me to talk about Harry, or do you want to ask questions?"

"We'll probably have some questions later," Lou said, "but why don't you tell us about Harry?"

"Well, like most folks up here, he was a character. Harry seemed to always say the wrong thing. I often shook my head as soon as he opened his mouth. He really should have taken one of those 'How to win friends and influence people' classes. He just never learned tact, never understood how not to put his foot in his mouth. So, being that way, he angered more people than he charmed. Actually, the word 'charm' was not in his vocabulary. But, if you got to know him, like I did, and like

George, Donny, and his grandson Todd did, you couldn't help but like the guy."

Jack interrupted. "Did he have any enemies? I don't mean someone who simply didn't like him, but an enemy who hated him and might be aggressive if given the chance?"

"No, as far as I know, he didn't have any enemies," Buck replied. "But you either liked the guy or you didn't. There wasn't any middle ground."

"Please continue," Lou said.

"He was an auctioneer, and a good one. While he didn't have a charming personality, he had excellent business sense. People knew he was fair and above-board. He never took advantage of people.

"Let's see—what else to tell you?" Buck said, wondering for a few seconds. "Well, he always wore a Chicago White Sox baseball cap," Buck said, grinning. "That thing got so dirty, we thought if it ever hit the floor, it would take off running. It smelled and was as dirty as a cap could be. He also wore bib overalls. In winter he wore flannel, but in summer he wore a plain shirt, and a mud-covered pair of hiking boots. I think he went to church a few times, but he didn't own a suit. He would probably wear a sweater. He couldn't have had much of a water bill, because I doubt he took a bath more than once a month and he didn't shave. Don't know how Estelle could stand him. That's about all I can say. He was just a tough-looking, tough-talking, and rough-living guy."

"Good description. Thanks," Lou replied, before asking his question. "Now let me repeat Jack's question and cut right to the chase. What do you think happened to Harry Moody?"

"Murdered," Buck said, without a second's hesitation.

"You didn't need to think about that answer?" Lou asked, surprised at the quick response.

"It *had* to be murder. Nothin' else it could be. He sure didn't run away. Some people thought he just up and left Estelle and went to where it was warmer. Well, I'm here to tell you, he didn't leave Estelle, and he didn't go to a warmer climate."

"Could he have had an accident and fallen through the ice?" Jack asked.

"No way! Harry was an outdoorsman from when he was a kid. He knew the water, ice, and the woods. Besides, if he fell through the ice, how would his wallet with money in it get into the woods?"

"Okay, let's assume he was murdered. Who could've killed him?" Lou asked.

"His son, Junior Moody."

"And his motive?" Jack asked.

"Well, let's just say that Harry and his son didn't get along. Harry definitely favored his daughter Norah to Junior. Then, too, Harry was of the opinion that Junior was not raising Todd to be a man. Junior didn't like hunting and fishing. All he wanted was for his son to read books and study. Harry offered

Todd a different life, and Junior didn't like his father trying to raise his son."

"Did the police investigate Junior?" Lou asked. "Did he have an alibi?"

"I don't know—you'd have to ask the police. I'm just saying that, if I had to pick a murderer, it would be Junior Moody, with no second choices."

"We appreciate your talking to us, Buck. Don Stewart refused to talk with us. Do you know any reason why he wouldn't want to talk about Harry?" Lou asked.

"That's just Donny. He's an emotional type. Harry's disappearance hit him hard, and he took a long time to accept it and move on. I think your investigation opens it up again, and he just doesn't want to recall his memories. Don't take it personally, and don't be thinking he's a suspect. He's quiet and, well, like I said, that's just Donny."

"Did Harry have a shanty on the lake?" Jack asked.

"We all had shanties. They were like our second homes in the winter."

Lou changed tack. "What can you tell us about George Zink? We understand he doesn't live in the area."

"The four of us were drinkin' buddies, fishin' buddies, and huntin' buddies. Zink became a snowbird after his wife convinced him to move to one of those retirement communities in Florida. When Harry died, George just clammed up." Buck continued. "Some of us thought maybe George had a psychological problem, you know, where people just stop talking? Well, that was George. It was weird. He'd come in to drink with Donny and me, and he'd just sit there with a blank expression on his face. It was crazy—made us uncomfortable. We'd talk to him, but he'd just stare, have a couple of beers, and then go home. I haven't heard anything about him since he moved to Florida."

"Do you know where he lives?" Jack asked.

"Clearwater rings a bell. I think the place is called Top of America, or something like that. You should be able to find it on the Internet. My wife sends them a Christmas card, and his wife sends us one. I could get you an address, if you want it."

"Yes, we'd appreciate that," Lou replied. "Thanks. You've been helpful, Buck."

CHAPTER
THREE

Since they were in Houghton Lake, Lou decided to contact Todd Moody to report what he had learned so far. But when he called the number Todd had given him he got a recording: "The number you have dialed is not in service. Please check the number and try again." Lou checked the business card and the number on his Blackberry; the numbers were the same. "This is odd," Lou thought, and then explained to Jack what had happened.

"Is there an address on the card?" Jack asked.

"Two, actually—a Houghton Lake post office box and a street address."

"The post office can't be far from here," Jack replied. "Let's go there first and then drive to the residence."

Lou parked in front of the post office and Jack got out. "I'll go in and check it out." A few minutes later he climbed back into Lou's car and said, "There is no P.O. Box with that number."

"This isn't making any sense," Lou responded. "I'll activate the GPS to find out where he lives, but my guess is the address is bogus as well."

Lou dutifully followed the audio and visual directions given by the GPS, but when they reached the address they found only a vacant lot.

"What is going *on* here?" Lou exclaimed.

"Are you sure you didn't *dream* about these people paying you a visit?" Jack asked.

"It was not a dream. It really happened."

"Then why would the guy give you a card full of false information?"

"I have no idea."

"Why don't you try the e-mail address?" Jack suggested.

"It can't hurt. Probably there's no e-mail, either."

Lou typed the e-mail address into his Blackberry. He wrote, "Hi Todd, I am in town looking into your grandfather's case. Can we meet? Regards to Mary. Lou Searing."

Within seconds, a response came through. "Hi, Lou. Glad you're working on the case. Would like to see you, but I don't want to be seen *with* you. Meet me in the parking lot at the MacMullen Center. Follow the signs after you leave I-75 about ten miles or so north of M-55. See you in a half-hour unless you can't make it. Todd."

Lou showed the message to Jack who handed the Blackberry back to Lou and asked, "Do you know where this place is?"

"In my past life as an administrator with the State, we held several meetings at the MacMullen Center," Lou replied. "It's a short drive north."

"Then let's go! We need to get some answers from this guy," Jack said, as Lou pulled away.

❋❄❋❄❋

Word was getting around Houghton Lake that Michigan's foremost private detective and his assistant were looking into the Moody case. Asking questions in a popular bar, a restaurant, and the festival office was sure to do it, and Lou and Jack welcomed it. The next step would be to put an article in the Resorter, the local weekly paper, explaining in greater detail Lou and Jack's mission to answer the question that had lingered for 25 years—what happened to Harry Moody? The talk and a newspaper article could easily evoke memories that would lead to clues, tips, and eventually a resolution.

❋❄❋❄❋

As Lou pulled into the MacMullen Center parking lot, he looked for a Hummer, but instead he saw a huge bus-like mobile home. Todd climbed down from the bus, welcomed

Lou and Jack, and invited them into his "home on wheels." Todd served his guests hot coffee and cookies.

"These cookies don't come close to Carol's, but at least they're something to dunk into the hot coffee," Todd said, playing host.

"Thank you. No such thing as a bad chocolate chip cookie!" Lou said.

"I'm glad you kept trying to reach me. I apologize for the distractions on the business card, but they're necessary, and I'll explain."

"Before you do that, tell me about your ride home from Grand Haven the night of the storm."

"It was a challenge, believe me. I was the last vehicle a state trooper allowed to travel on eastbound I-96 at exit 10, and that was only because I drove the Hummer. He asked me to report any stranded motorists and not to take any risks. There were several whiteouts, but we made it. Once we got to Grand Rapids, conditions improved."

"Good. I've been curious about whether you had to spend the night in a church or with the Red Cross. Now, why no phone, residence, or P.O. Box?"

"Harassment."

"After all these years?" Jack asked.

"It started again about a year ago," Todd explained. "That's the major reason I asked you to solve Harry's disappearance, to explain what happened."

"Why are you being harassed, and by whom?" Lou asked.

"Donny Stewart is the main reason for the harassment. He was one of my grandfather's fishing and hunting buddies."

"His name has come up," Lou said. "He refused to talk with us."

"Of course he refused, and he will try to make your life miserable for taking on this case."

"And here I thought I finally had a case where I wouldn't have to dodge bullets or barricade my home in Grand Haven," Lou sighed.

"I don't think you'll have those problems, but it won't be a cakewalk."

"So, why do you tolerate the harassment? Why don't you just drive your motor home to Florida and start a new life?" Jack asked.

"I believe Donny is convinced that my dad and I killed his good friend."

"We've learned that your dad may have had reason not to be fond of Harry," Lou began. "But, we also got the impression that Harry took you under his wing—taught you to hunt and fish."

"That's true, but after I matured a bit, I became involved with animal rights and became an advocate for PETA. Well, before Harry disappeared, I was a pain to hunters and fishermen in the area. I carried placards defending deer and other wildlife when I would confront hunters and fishermen. They were upset with my posters, which had photos of deer being gutted and pictures of kids hunting with the caption 'Your Children are Killers!'—things like that."

"I can imagine you weren't the most popular man up here where fishing and hunting are important to the economy," Lou said, shaking his head.

"'Not popular' hardly describes it. I was often threatened. You didn't see a house at the address on my card. When my home burned, it was basically a drill for the local fire department."

"Someone set the fire?" Jack asked.

"I don't know. It was one of those, 'If nobody talks, nobody is blamed' things."

"I must give you credit for standing up for your principles, but life sure would have been a lot simpler if you had taken your cause to downtown Detroit, for example."

"I know, but I wasn't playing a game. I truly believed what I was preaching. Discretion would have been the better part of valor, because I'm not sure my ranting and raving saved one animal or a single fish."

"You got rid of your phone number because of the harassment, right?"

"Oh, yeah! And the post office box was full of hate mail. My e-mail was okay because I could delete what I didn't want."

"So, you live in and out of this motor home? Where's the Hummer?" Jack asked.

"I'm always in one vehicle or the other. I store the unused vehicle in a pole barn that belongs to the Humane Society."

"Okay, that's not a great way to live, but it's where you are right now," Lou summarized. "Now I'd like information about Harry. I should have asked you this when you were in my home, but obvious as it is, I didn't. Who killed Harry?"

"I don't know. I mean, I have an idea, but I do not know. It was not me, nor my dad."

"An article in the local paper said he told friends he was about to come into a lot of money. What was that about?" Lou asked.

"I don't know. My dad mentioned that often, referring to the newspaper article, but we never knew where that comment came from."

"No rich uncles in the Moody family?" Jack asked.

"Not that I'm aware of."

"Did Harry gamble?" Lou asked.

"When he and his buddies played cards in the bar, he could ante with the best of them, but I never heard of anything substantial."

"Was there anyone who owed him a great deal of money? You know, maybe he loaned a bundle at one time?" Jack asked.

"Could be, but it'd be news to me."

"So, we conclude you can't help us regarding who might have killed your gramps. I mean, you don't even have a hunch?" Lou asked.

"No. I do recall my grandma saying something about Gramps being at the bottom of Houghton Lake. My dad asked why she thought that, and she said, "Because if he was alive, he'd have made his way home, by hook or by crook!" He didn't come home, so she knew he was dead. And since his body had not been found, either in the water or on land, she figured he had to be at the bottom of the lake."

"Maybe he is," Jack mused.

"As far as I know, nobody asked the authorities to dive that spring, and back then, they didn't have those sonar devices to pick up objects under water. Plus, it was the middle of winter, so Gramps wouldn't have fallen into the lake."

"Could he have been pushed down a fishing hole?" Jack asked.

"No auger on the face of the earth could make a hole big enough for him to fall into. I do know that snowmobilers spent hours on the lake looking for him, and they certainly would have found a hole big enough for Gramps to slip into."

"I think that's enough for today," Lou stated. Say 'hello' to Mary for me."

"I will. Mary has been a life-long friend. In fact, it was a friend of hers who was married last weekend in Grand Haven."

"Speaking of your visit to Grand Haven," Lou began. "Why do I hear that I should be cautious of you, that you and Mary invade homes?"

"That's part of a quarter-century of harassment. I've never broken into a home in my life. Why would I? My assets exceed ten million dollars. If I want something, I buy it."

"And, it seems to me that if you wanted to buy a solution to your grandfather's murder, you could."

"I imagine I could, but I want it explained by a highly-respected detective, who always gets it right. You're that person, which is why I came to you."

"Okay," Lou said. "We're going to go back to Houghton Lake to talk with the newspaper editor, and then your grandmother, we hope. We'll stay in touch."

"Thanks, Lou, and you, too, Jack."

As Lou and Jack stepped off the motor home into the bitter cold air, Lou said softly, "Get the license plate number. I'm not really sure about this guy."

"Will do," Jack replied, moving toward the back of the motor home on a circular route to Lou's car. "I'll also take a photo of this bus."

As Lou pulled out of the parking lot, he remarked, "I get strange vibes, Jack, just a bizarre feeling. I add up the numbers, but I never get the same sum. This guy may not be as innocent as he seems."

"If he's that wealthy, why doesn't he get out of the area?" Jack asked. "And who in his right mind would subject himself to years of harassment? I mean, if someone really did burn down his home, what would keep them from torching the bus, or planting a car bomb? I agree, this isn't making much sense."

✳✳✳✳✳

Lou and Jack sat in wooden chairs in the editor's office of the Houghton Lake Resorter. The editor, Max Royster, seemed to be an old-time newspaper man, not in actual age, but experienced in production of a weekly.

Lou explained what they hoped to learn from Max.

"Well, I never thought this day would come," Max said, leaning back in his old-fashioned armchair. "The answer to my prayers now sits in my office,"

"Meaning?" Jack asked.

"Time flies, and Harry Moody's disappearance seems like yesterday. That mystery lies on Houghton Lake's history like a sore that never healed. I've long hoped someone with extensive investigating experience could solve the mystery so we could stop wondering what happened to Harry."

"Well, we may solve it," Lou replied. "But, this is our first cold case, so we've no track-record in this type of investigation."

"Today or twenty-five years ago, the crime still has all the components: victim, unknown motive and weapon, witnesses, clues, so I think it wouldn't be too different. Sure, time obscures memory, and clues collect dust, but if anyone can cut through all of that, it's you and Jack."

"I appreciate your confidence in our skills. We think you can help us through your newspaper."

"You tell me what you need, and you'll have it," Max replied.

"I'd like you to publish a series of articles over the next few weeks," Lou said.

"Be glad to. Oh, sorry," Max said, rising. "I'm not being a good host. Can I get you some coffee?"

Lou and Jack nodded, and Jack said, "Thanks. We both like it black, with no sugar."

As Max headed for the coffee pot, he said, "What kind of articles were you thinking of?"

"I see the first one as historical," Lou began. "It's been 25 years since a citizen mysteriously disappeared during the Tip-Up Town Festival. Remind readers of what happened, then introduce us as being new on the case. Conclude with an editorial that basically says it is time to solve the mystery and remove the albatross from Houghton Lake's neck. Encourage anyone with information to contact us. We'll come back and set up an interview room at the Holiday Inn where people can talk with us."

"Sounds good!" Max returned to his desk and started scribbling on a yellow legal pad.

"The second article would concern Harry," Lou continued. "It would inform your readers about Harry's description, his personality, his auction business. Sort of profile him, maybe get recollections of him from his buddies."

"And repeat the plea for people to come forward with information?" Max asked.

"Right."

"And the third article?" Max asked.

"By then we should have more information, so you can update your readers on our investigation."

"I've got an idea," Jack interjected. "Money talks. I suggest we offer a lot of money, say ten thousand dollars, to anyone who provides information leading to a solution of the case."

"Who has that kind of money, if someone *does* provide that information?" Max asked.

"We'll find it," Lou replied, adding, "You just put the offer in big letters and enclose it in a box in the middle of your article."

"Okay, will do." Max shook his head dubiously as he made a note.

"Before we leave, we'd like to hear from you. What do you think happened to Harry Moody?" Lou asked.

"I think his mistake was to tell his buddies he was coming into money. But he had a reputation for saying the wrong thing at the wrong time. I think that was true—his coming into money—but I don't think his wife or any family member knew about it. So, when he got the money, he realized he would have a whole new life if he moved on, so he did just that."

"Moved on?" Jack asked.

"Yeah, probably to Colorado where it's a real heaven for fishermen and hunters."

"So, you don't think he was murdered?" Lou asked.

"Nah, murder doesn't happen here—it just doesn't."

"How do you explain the wallet in the woods?" Jack asked.

"Harry was a lot smarter than people gave him credit for. He was smart enough to be a successful businessman. I suspect Harry left the wallet in the woods because, with a great deal of money, he didn't need cash or credit cards. And if he changed his identity, what good was his old license? That was a deliberate act to convince the police he was killed or kidnapped. I think he's sitting in a bar in some mountain community, enjoying life to the fullest."

"You could be right," Lou replied.

"Have you heard of Norah Moody?"

"Only that she was Harry's favored child?" Lou replied.

"She's Harry and Estelle's adopted daughter who is mentally retarded. Harry, despite his gruff exterior, had a soft heart for those like her, too. He hoped to save enough money to build an apartment complex for people with disabilities. Harry insisted that his estate should all go to Norah so she would have care for the rest of her life, but Estelle was concerned for her own financial future, and while she loved Norah, she and Harry were always at odds about his demand."

"Why would he leave his retarded daughter?" Jack asked.

"His concern was that she be cared for for the rest of her life, and he could do that by leaving some of his new-found wealth. He didn't need to be in Houghton Lake to help her."

"You make a compelling case for a 'runaway' explanation," Lou said.

"But, if he didn't skip town and was murdered, who could have done it?" Jack asked.

"This is way out there, but it is possible that Estelle and Junior put their heads together and found a way to kill him."

"Because?" Jack asked.

"I know love overcomes all things, but let's face it—Harry was not a joy to be around. He smelled, had an unlovable personality, and spent most of his time hunting, fishing, and drinking. His home was cluttered with all kinds of junk. He was a great auctioneer, but he couldn't pass up whatever he thought was a deal, so he'd buy anything dirt cheap. He'd plan to auction it later, but by then, he considered it a treasure."

"You've certainly given us a lot to think about," Lou said. "Thanks for the coffee. Here's my card, if you need to contact me. We'll plan to be back within a week, but I trust that if you get any responses from your readers you'll forward them to me. My e-mail address is on there, too."

"I most certainly will. Nice meeting you two. You've quite a reputation to uphold."

"As far as some folks are concerned, I guess," Lou replied.

Jack rose and shook Max's hand. "You've been a great help and I suspect will be of help in the future.

Then in the manner of Lieutenant Colombo's famous "One more question..." Lou said, "Todd Moody—what can you tell us about him?"

"You don't want anything to do with him, Lou," Max replied without any hesitation.

"Why do you say that?" Lou asked.

"Let's just say he's not the brightest nut on the bolt, if you know what I mean."

"Please explain."

"You could write a book about Todd Moody; very smooth, very odd, a master manipulator! Everything he says is a lie, or it needs to be taken with a *carton* of Morton salt."

"Lives in a motor home, we understand," Jack remarked off-handedly.

"Oh, give me a break! The guy has a castle in Roscommon."

"Did he build it with insurance money after his home here burned?" Lou asked.

"He never lived here, and no home of his ever burned. Where did you get that?"

"Just picked it up in our research," Lou said, not wanting to divulge his source.

Max was adamant. "He's a pathological liar, Lou. You can't believe a word he tells you."

"He's Harry Moody's grandson?" Jack asked.

"Yes, I believe that's true."

"He was an animal rights activist, right?" Lou asked.

"You mean when he wasn't in jail for poaching?" Max asked, with a chuckle.

"Why do you suppose he might ask me to work on this case?" Lou asked.

"If he did, I really don't know. Nobody can explain anything he says or does."

The phone rang in the newspaper office and Max punched a button on his desk console. "Excuse me; this could be a news-worthy call."

"Sure."

Max answered the phone and within seconds, turned back to Lou and Jack. "That was Todd Moody with a message for you. He says his grandmother is not feeling well and won't be able to talk with you."

"That's odd. I'm at the point where I don't believe one word that comes from that guy's mouth," Lou said, shaking his head. Then Lou took his cell phone and dialed the number he had for Estelle Moody.

"Hello."

"Mrs. Moody. This is Lou Searing calling. We're on our way to see you."

"Mr. Searing, I'm not well. Guess I've got a virus or food poisoning. Didn't Todd call to cancel our meeting when you finished with Max?"

"Yes, he did."

"I'll be happy to talk with you in a few days when I'm feeling better."

"That's fine. Take care of yourself."

As Lou put his phone away, he said to Jack and Max, "That was Estelle Moody and I guess Todd was right. She is too ill to meet with us. Perhaps it will be clearer one day," Lou said. "We're on our way back to west Michigan, but we'll be in touch as we see this through."

"It's a pleasure to work with you," Max said, walking the two to the front door.

The drive to Grand Haven was hazardous, the roads icy in spots. After a few whiteouts, the flashing lights of county plows meant sand or salt was at work to make the driving safer.

Lou and Jack pronounced the initial visit to Houghton Lake most successful, but they were indeed happy to be in the comfort of their homes.

CHAPTER
FOUR

JANUARY 15TH

Lou confirmed that Todd lived in a fashionable home in Roscommon. And when he checked with the Houghton Lake Fire Department to find out if Todd's former home had actually burned down, there was no record of such a fire.

Jack tackled the mystery surrounding Todd's lying. On the Internet he found considerable material and discussion about pathological lying. The behavior begins in childhood and stabilizes in the teen years, so Jack contacted the Houghton Lake School District Administrative Office and asked to speak to a counselor. When a Mr. Leon Williams answered, Jack explained that he was investigating the disappearance of Harry Moody, Todd's grandfather, and that he would like to talk to someone who knew and perhaps had worked with Todd when he was in school.

Mr. Williams replied, "That would be me, for one. I taught history before becoming a counselor, and Todd was in a couple of my classes."

"I don't mean you should violate confidentiality, but can you tell me if he lied frequently in school?" Jack asked.

"Yes, he did, and it was quite serious. Honestly, I don't think he realized he was doing it, but he was a loner because of it. People quickly learned that you never knew when he was speaking the truth or telling a lie."

"Where did he graduate in his class?"

"Upper third. He was very smart. He may have been lying when he talked, but he listened carefully and could process information adequately and then respond correctly in testing situations."

"What did he do after graduation?" Jack asked.

"He graduated from Harvard. Then he became a nuclear scientist with NASA. From what I understand, his employer knew of his condition, but his work was exceptional. Data can't lie, so his contribution to the space program brought him millions in compensation."

"And yet he chooses to live in mid-Michigan, when he could live anywhere?" Jack asked.

"I can't explain that. Maybe familiarity is important to him," Leon replied.

"Thanks for your help, Mr. Williams," Jack said sincerely.

❄❄❄❄❄

JANUARY 18

At mid-week, Lou and Jack met at Russ's Family Restaurant in Grand Haven. Jack shared what he had learned from the Internet about pathological liars and he described his conversation with Leon Williams.

Lou wanted to brainstorm. With hot black coffee in front of them, Lou began, "Let's talk about the money. What could be the source of the 'easy money' Harry mentioned to his friends?"

"Lottery winnings? The lottery was up and running in 1985," Jack replied.

"He could have spotted something valuable among items he was to auction and kept it for himself," Lou suggested.

"He could have heard from an attorney that he was going to receive a huge inheritance from a long-lost uncle," Jack hinted with a grin. Lou frowned and shook his head, prompting Jack to respond, "Hey, you wanted ideas! It *could* have happened."

"I suppose you're right," Lou said with a smile.

"Or, maybe he heard about a fortune and decided to steal it," Jack said. "It could really be that simple."

"And, the one whose fortune was stolen knocked Harry off for revenge," Lou said. "Is that what you're thinking?"

"Yes, that's one of a hundred scenarios."

Lou's cell phone rang. "Excuse me, I want to get this."

"Lou, this is Max in Houghton Lake."

"Yes, Max. What's on your mind?" Lou looked hopefully at Jack.

"Well, yesterday's article mentioned the reward, and I put in a photo of Harry. I got a call from a man named Bob Adams, who was about ten years old in 1985. The spring of '86, this Adams says he found a Chicago White Sox baseball cap at the lakeshore that looks like the one Harry is wearing in the photo. He didn't say anything because he didn't know anyone was looking for the cap or its owner. The ball cap has been in his baseball collection since he found it."

"I need to follow protocol and get that hat to the Police so they can enter it into their collection of evidence," Lou said, mindful of procedures that must be followed. "I expect the Chief will allow me to request a DNA analysis."

"Makes sense."

"Sounds like the newspaper article worked! E-mail me how to reach this Bob Adams, and we'll talk with him when we get back to Houghton Lake."

"Okay, does that mean Harry was underwater?" Max asked.

"It's logical," Lou replied, "but that's only one scenario. The cap might not be Harry's. It could have blown from land onto the ice, and when the ice melted, the cap was in the water."

"Oh, yeah, I see. I guess I should have figured that out," Max admitted.

"No problem. You're a newspaperman who gathers facts. It's our job to take the facts, test them, and then make them prove themselves against a number of possibilities."

"I wanted you to have the word ASAP," Max said, still a bit embarrassed at having jumped to a conclusion.

"I'm glad you did. It may well be worth ten thousand dollars to Mr. Adams."

❄❄❄❄❄

Lou and Jack decided that a weekend visit to Houghton Lake was necessary. But for some reason, they hadn't realized that the upcoming weekend was the Tip-Up Town Festival.

"Well, I guess we'll have a unique experience after all, Lou," Jack said.

"Maybe if we pretend it's 1985, we'll stumble onto something helpful."

"Makes sense to me."

Lou picked up the tab, left a generous tip, and the two headed to their respective homes.

❄❄❄❄❄

Upon their return home from Russ's, both Lou and Jack went online to see what Tip-Up Town was all about. They each typed "Tip-Up Town Festival" into their search boxes, and after opening the site, got the immediate impression that a lot of tom foolery takes place. The list of events included a cross-dressing contest, a polar bear dip, frozen-turkey bowling, snowmobile races on the lake, a parade, and a craft show. Tip-Up Town also elects a mayor and a festival queen each year. And, it goes without saying that a lot of beer is consumed in and around shanties as the fishermen have a good time celebrating a popular pastime in the dead of winter.

❄❄❄❄❄

JANUARY 19

As the men traveled east, Jack brought up the White Sox baseball cap.

"Do you think the State Police Lab could pick up DNA on that cap?" Jack asked. "It's been 25 years, and the cap was found in the lake."

"Maybe," Lou replied. "Their technology is amazing."

"My guess is that the DNA would stay on the item," Jack said, "but ice and water could have corrupted it."

"Okay, let's assume the cap did belong to Harry," Lou said.

"Then, I'd say we snagged a great clue," Jack stated. "It puts Harry near the lake."

"Exactly," Lou replied.

"Tell me again what your plan is for today," Jack asked.

"Max put in the paper in bold print that we'll be at the Holiday Inn Express. People who want to talk with us can come to the motel without causing comment in town. It's hard to predict how many will come. If several people show up, some will talk with you and some with me. If we have only one or two, we can both talk to them. If we're lucky, someone will have seen or heard something relevant. Maybe it's been on his or her mind for a long time, and now it's time to tell someone."

"Houghton Lake is a small community and word travels quickly," Jack mused. "People are probably discussing the chance to participate in solving Harry's disappearance."

"Good point."

❄❄❄❄❄

When the men pulled into the Holiday Inn Express around ten a.m., they planned to spend the night and continue their investigation the next day. Each got a room, and Lou arranged with the manager to set up a room for the interviews and to have coffee available.

At noon, the manager assured Lou that all was ready. "We've already received a few calls about your visit. Oh, I almost forgot, a gentleman dropped off a ball hat. He said you are welcome to call, but he has nothing to say beyond his having found this cap in the water. He said he didn't want it back. The cap is in my office."

"Thanks." Lou replied, pleased to hear that some people were planning to come forward.

"Yes. You may be quite busy."

When Lou entered his room, the message light was already blinking on the phone beside the bed. The front-desk receptionist directed him to a recording, so Lou made sure his hearing aids were turned on, then punched the access code to the message.

"Mr. Searing, this is June Jacobs. I was mayor of Tip-Up Town when Harry Moody disappeared. I have information for you, but I don't want anyone to know I'm meeting with you. Believe me, this is important. If you'll call me for a private conversation, I think I can aid you in your investigation." June concluded her recorded message with thanks to Lou and Jack for working on the case before leaving her phone number.

As Lou put up signs in the lobby directing people to the conference room he looked to his right and saw Todd Moody. "Good to see you, Todd."

"Thank you for bringing your investigation into the community," Todd said.

"You're welcome. Solving a difficult case requires information from a variety of sources, and Jack and I hope to get some good leads this afternoon."

"You may be surprised how many citizens come in to help."

"Todd, would you mind stepping into the conference room for a few minutes, so we can talk? The interviews won't begin for another half hour."

"Sure," Todd said. The two walked to the room, and Lou closed the door behind them.

"Have a seat," Lou said, pointing to a comfortable chair. "I have a question."

"Sure."

"Todd, we've done some investigating and have learned that you have not been honest with us. In fact, you've told some whopping stories. What do you say to this?"

"I don't know what you mean."

"There are inconsistencies between what you told us and what we've learned."

"What, for example?" Todd asked.

"You say that you live out of your motor home and park the Hummer at the Humane Society's pole barn. But you actually live in a quite elegant home in Roscommon. And the Humane Society has no pole barn."

Todd simply stared at his clenched hands.

"I can give several other examples if you like."

"I'm sorry. I'd like to leave, Mr. Searing."

"Of course you can leave. I just want the truth. You asked me to take time from my life to help you. I agreed, but I expect— even demand—that you be honest with me. Otherwise, I can't help you. You see, it's my job as an investigator to figure out what is true and what isn't. It's the only way to give the authorities a solution to the crime that I can stand behind."

Todd stood up. "Thank you for working to solve the murder of my grandfather," he said. Then he grabbed and shook Lou's hand and quickly walked out of the room, leaving Lou shaking his head in bewilderment.

Lou decided that he should consult a psychiatrist to learn how to handle Todd. Maybe he shouldn't have been so direct, but on the other hand, Lou couldn't be bothered with a liar. He had no experience with someone on the right side of the law being so dishonest. Lou walked from the conference room to make sure the coffee was ready and that the signs indicating the conference room were clearly visible. Jack appeared with his attaché, pen, and notepad, like a grad student headed to a seminar.

"Jack, I'd like you to register people and get their contact information—whatever they are comfortable giving: telephone numbers, e-mail, home addresses. Ask general questions like, 'What kind of information do you have for us?' Assure them of confidentiality. I'll try to move people through without missing the gist of what they're telling us."

"I understand," Jack said, settling into a chair outside the conference room. "Do you want full privacy while you are with a guest?"

"If you need to talk with me, you can come in, but I don't want another guest interrupting. I'll send our guests out the other door of the room so people won't encounter each other."

As the clock in the lobby struck two, no one had approached Lou and Jack. They agreed the interviews had been a good idea, but either no one had information, or no one wanted to share what they knew.

Alone in the large room, Lou called June Jacobs, the mayor from 1985. "This is Lou Searing, returning your call. I'm working on the Moody case."

"Yes, thanks for calling. I hope my phone line is not tapped."

"We can meet somewhere, if you wish," Lou offered.

"No, I'll take the risk. First of all, thank you for looking into this case. If you solve this, the City Council will probably name a street in your honor."

"The satisfaction of solving it is all I need. What do you have for us?" Lou asked, wanting to get on with the purpose of the call.

"The mayor and several members of the Council were given certain information about Harry at the time of his disappearance. The Chamber of Commerce asked us not to direct attention to Harry, for the emphasis needed to be on the Festival and all that Houghton Lake offers tourists. So, we kept quiet. Shortly afterward, two council members received death threats: they mustn't release information to the media, or to the police. Needless to say, that shut people up, and what we knew froze like a block of ice."

"And, you'll tell me what you know?" Lou asked, hoping to get to the point.

"Yes, as long as you assure me that you will not broadcast what you hear."

"I will do my best," Lou promised.

"That's not good enough, Mr. Searing. I need assurance no one will hear about this, and certainly not that it was I you heard it from."

"As I said, I'll do my best. Legalities may compel me to tell a judge or jury, but I will not pass on your information unnecessarily."

"I guess I'll have to take the risk."

Lou sighed quietly. "Thank you."

June began. "Shortly after Harry was reported missing, we were told that the motive for his death was that he was about to claim a pot of gold."

"Like at the end of a rainbow?" Lou asked, with a hint of sarcasm.

"This pot of gold was real, and worth millions. Someone had visited him for an appraisal of gold coins and bars. This person planned to sell the cache, but he needed an honest accounting. The story was assumed to be true because Harry had done a lot of appraising in his auctioning business."

"What do you mean that Harry was going to 'claim' the pot of gold."

"Steal it." June replied without hesitation.

"And he was killed during the theft?"

"That's what I understood. But, it's confusing because Harry, for all of his lack of tact, was an honest man. So, stealing was totally out of character for him."

"Who owned the gold?" Lou asked.

"I don't know."

"Did you get the impression it was someone he knew, or at least someone in town?"

"Nothing was said about the owner. I doubt he lived in Houghton Lake."

"Could the owner be Todd Moody?" Lou asked. "He is quite wealthy."

"Todd Moody? That nut who lives in the motor home and protests hunting?"

"Yes."

"Todd is a lot of things, but wealthy is not one of them. He inherited the motor home from his father. I don't think Todd has earned an honest dollar in his life."

"He also can't seem to tell the truth from a lie?" Lou asked.

"It is sad, Lou. The kid never grew up or learned to relate to people. He's sort of the town mental case. He's picked-on and humiliated."

"Okay, that's enough, thank you," Lou replied. "Your comments may be instrumental in our bringing justice to Harry."

"Or maybe only an explanation. Somehow, I don't think justice will be the outcome." June ended the call.

While Lou was on the phone, Jack had greeted two people. Lou opened the door and Jack brought the first visitor in to meet Lou, introducing her as Rebecca Harding, then closing the door on his way out.

"Hello. I'm Lou Searing. I'm pleased to meet you."

"Thank you, the pleasure is mine," Rebecca replied. "I love your books. I've read them all and can't wait for the next one. I brought four of them with me—would you autograph them before I leave?"

"Certainly. But I hope you didn't come here just to get autographs, much as my ego would like to think so."

"You'll have to be the judge of how relevant my observations are, but I'm sure this session will be much more to my liking than yours."

"What do you have for me?" Lou asked, eager to get the interview going.

"One sentence sums it up: Todd Moody is the world's most successful conman."

"We understand he tells some whoppers," Lou replied.

"I'm a middle-school psychologist. I saw Todd in my office at school on many occasions, and over time I learned that he is extremely intelligent. You know how some people are prodigies and can play the piano with great skill at a young age? Or others are idiot savants who can tell you the day of any date in the history of the calendar? Well, I am convinced that Todd is like that, controlling people with words. When I researched his condition, I discovered that people who behave this way are very insecure and they get satisfaction from controlling their listeners."

"Is it pathological?" Lou asked. "Does he realize he's lying? Does he know most people are on to him and don't believe a word he says?"

"Yes, I believe he's in control at all times. He creates his own world."

"Was Harry really his grandfather?"

"Yes."

"Did he attend Harvard?"

"Yes, that's a fact."

"Did he work for NASA?"

"Yes, he did."

"Did Harry try to raise Todd to be like him?"

"Yes, and while I can't be absolutely sure, I believe being in the middle of a conflict between his father and grandfather caused his problem. His dad and his Gramps were as different as two adults could be. Todd, to survive being with both, had to make up stories, because if he told the truth, it angered one or the other, and sustained the conflict. Like a kid going through his parents' divorce, Todd was the ball tossed back and forth between grandfather and father. It got to the point where Todd believed that he was the reason for their hatred." It appeared Rebecca had had considerable contact with a young Todd.

"Did Todd carry placards against hunting?"

"Yes. People shouted threats, threw things at him, some kids even knocked him down and kicked him. Very sad, Lou."

"Why didn't he just leave town?" Lou asked.

"That's the one thing I could never figure out. Punishment usually results in escape or aggression; but he turned to neither, which might explain his mental health. Maybe he was incapable of making that decision or of carrying it out."

"Did Todd kill Harry?" Lou asked outright.

"No, I'm sure he didn't."

"How about Harry's son, Junior? Did he kill his father?"

"I think he did. I'm convinced that if that happened, and if Todd *knew* his father killed his grandfather, it could only add to his mental problems."

"Junior has died, correct?" Lou asked.

"According to Todd he did, but I'm not sure of that. Junior left Houghton Lake a long time ago. He couldn't bear to see his son being mistreated by so many people."

"Can't say as I blame him. Do you know where he moved?"

"No, but I do know who was his best friend while he lived here: Josh Higbee. Like Junior, Josh is a quiet, keep-to-himself man. I wouldn't call him a hermit, but one rarely sees him in public."

"I'll try to contact him. Anything else?" Lou asked.

"If you'll sign my books, I'll be on my way. I'm confident you'll solve this, and when you do, this community will heave a collective sigh of relief."

Lou signed each book, shook Rebecca's hand, and thanked her for coming.

❄❄❄❄❄

Jack took the opportunity to talk with the second person waiting to see Lou. Lawrence Wilbur felt seeing Jack was sufficient, but Jack insisted he talk with Lou. So Lawrence walked into the conference room, shook Lou's hand, and sat down.

"Thank you for waiting," Lou said, apologetic for taking longer with Rebecca than he had expected.

"Not a problem. I told Jack all I know, but he wanted me to talk with you."

"Each of us might ask different questions. And, by wrapping two minds around what you say, we might better understand your experience," Lou explained.

"That makes sense."

"I'm all ears, Lawrence. What do you have for me?"

"I'm sort of the neighborhood watchdog—I know every-one's comings and goings. My neighbors sometimes make fun of me and my habit of knowing what is going on around me, but every once in a while it comes in handy."

"So, you saw something that might help us?"

"Yes, I did. In fact, I may have been one of the last people to see Harry Moody alive."

"Tell me about it," Lou said.

"Harry and Estelle lived across the street from me and a few houses to the south. Estelle still lives in their house. Now, Harry had two vehicles. His pickup was always filled with junk; well, I call it junk. I suppose others saw some value in it, but to me it was junk, related to his auction business, I assumed. The other vehicle was a snowmobile; he only took the snowmobile when he went ice fishing. The night he disappeared, I saw him drive past on his snowmobile."

"Are you certain it was Harry?" Lou asked.

"If you knew Harry, you wouldn't confuse him with anyone else. It was Harry."

"Okay, I'll accept that. What time of day was this?"

"I'd say mid to late afternoon. The next morning, the snow-mobile was back at his house, which would imply that he had come home," Lawrence continued. "But, Harry always—and I repeat, *always*—put a tarpaulin over the snowmobile. And that next morning, there was no tarp on the snowmobile."

"So, let me get this straight," Lou began. "As far as you are concerned, Harry Moody never came back that night. But someone, probably the killer or an accomplice, drove the snowmobile back to his home."

"Precisely my point," Lawrence said, nodding positively. "Conclusion number one: because he only took the snowmobile when he went ice fishing, I suspect Harry was killed between his home and his shanty. The snowmobile came home, which means Harry didn't drive it into a soft area of the lake and drown."

"Did you tell the police what you've told me?" Lou asked.

"Yes, but by then someone had found Harry's wallet in the woods. Well, I trust you know nothing else was found around the wallet when the snow melted. The police listened, but their minds seemed to be made up that Harry was kidnapped and taken from town."

"A White Sox baseball cap was found in the water in the spring," Lou said to Lawrence. "You are aware of that."

"Yes, and that's something else I have an opinion on. And by the way, Mr. Kelly didn't ask me this, so I guess your 'two heads are better than one' theory proved accurate. People will say Harry always wore his White Sox cap, that he was never seen without that cap. My observation is that he did not wear his White Sox cap when he took the snowmobile out to his shanty. The wind might blow it off, or if Harry hit a rough spot, it could flip off. And Harry cherished that hat, so he didn't want to risk losing it. Besides, he needed his parka hood, because driving a snowmobile is a downright chilling experience. Finally, it becomes warm fairly quickly in the shanty, because of the small space to heat, and a hat isn't needed for protection from the elements. Conclusion number two: Harry did not wear his White Sox cap the night he disappeared."

"That's it—two conclusions," Lawrence said firmly, nodding his head.

"Thank you very much. Your insights will be instrumental in solving this thing." The two men shook hands, and Lawrence left through the back door.

When Lou again ventured into the hall to see Jack, sitting next to him was Todd Moody. "Hello, Todd," Lou said, wondering why he would return so soon. Todd nodded.

"I thought I'd hang around and see how many people took advantage of the opportunity to meet with the two of you."

"As Jack no doubt told you, only two made the effort, but their observations will help us."

"Good."

"It is. Todd, did your father pass away, or is he still living?"

"Dad died several years ago."

"Where was he living when he died?"

"He and Mom had moved to southern Mississippi, to Biloxi. They liked being on or near the water, and like a lot of Michiganians, they wanted to be warm during the winter months. They got a condo with a view of the Gulf."

"Is your mom still living?"

"No, she died shortly after Dad. She couldn't take the loneliness, and she had heart disease."

Lou took down the information, fully realizing the likelihood that nothing Todd said was true.

Todd probably hadn't reached his motor home before Lou had Max Royster on the phone. "Hi Max, I need your help again."

"I'll help if I can, you know that."

"Did your paper print a death notice when Junior Moody passed? And, for Mrs. Moody, Junior's wife?"

"Let me check the archives on my computer. I should have it in a matter of seconds. Yes, the item is brief, but it is here. It was in a 1998 edition,

> *Harold Moody Jr., age 73, has died in Biloxi, Mississippi.*
> *Mr. Moody chose to be cremated, and no memorial service*
> *will be held. Friends may make memorial contributions to*
> *the Humane Society of Roscommon County.*

"Now, I'll put in his wife's name, and we'll see what comes up. There's nothing here, Lou. That doesn't mean she didn't die, but I probably would have heard about it if she had."

"Thanks, Max. I'll be back in touch."

Lou turned to Jack. "Now what do we make of this?"

"Same old thing; Todd has no credibility. We can't believe a word he says."

Lou nodded in agreement, then brightened. "I noticed they have free popcorn in the bar next door. Let's have a cold one with some popcorn and let what we've heard settle into our brains."

"Sounds like a plan."

Following the break for popcorn, Lou called Josh Higbee.

"Mr. Higbee, this is Lou Searing. I'm investigating the disappearance of Harry Moody back in 1985. May I visit with you and ask some questions? I understand you were a good friend of Junior Moody."

"I don't have anything to say."

"I have only a few questions."

"I realize that, but I don't have anything to say," Josh replied, and quietly hung up. The call was brief, resembling that of a phone solicitor interrupting a man enjoying dinner after a hard day at the office.

Lou would knock on Josh's door because he needed information about Junior. And so far, Josh appeared to be his best source.

CHAPTER
FIVE

JANUARY 18TH

If Lawrence Wilbur was correct in his observations about Harry Moody, and Lou had no reason to doubt him, Lou needed to understand life in a 'town' of fishing shanties, a world foreign to him. It was mid-to-late afternoon when Lou called Max asking if he could introduce him to a real ice fisherman, so he could visit a shanty and learn about life on the frozen lake.

Max called back to say a friend, Doris Winston, would welcome his visit. The air was cold and the bright sun provided excellent lighting that allowed good visibility. Lou had not brought warm enough clothes for a visit to a shanty far from shore, so thankfully, he could drive his car out onto the ice.

Lou had not been inside a shanty since his boyhood. He knocked on the door of what looked like a wooden closet and heard, "It's open!" which he took as an invitation to enter. He walked into a six-foot by eight-foot den. The focus was the fishing hole, a rectangular area of open water cut into about six inches of ice.

"Doris? I'm Lou Searing. Thank you for agreeing to help me understand life in a shanty."

"My pleasure," Doris replied. She was wearing a sweatshirt, brown overalls, and insulated boots. "Do you want some coffee, something cold, or perhaps a swig of brandy from my flask? Whatever makes you happy."

"I'll take a cup of coffee."

"It has to be black out here—I don't have sissy sugar or cream. So, you either drink it as is or wait till you get back to civilization."

"Black and strong is fine with me. It's the only way I'll drink it," Lou replied, trying to convince his hostess that he was also a tough character.

"Well, don't just stand there. Plop down on the two-seater! It might feel a little warm at first—I love to fish in the winter, but I don't like a cold butt—gotta draw the line somewhere. If it's uncomfortable, I'll turn it off."

"Warm is good," Lou replied.

"So, is this your first visit to a shanty?" Doris asked, handing Lou a small cup of coffee from a thermos.

"I went ice fishing with my uncle when I was a boy, but that was sixty-plus years ago."

"Well, it hasn't changed much. Still takes a hole in the ice, a cozy little house, a fishing pole, some bait, and a warm seat."

"I'll bet you have some new technology today, though," Lou said.

"What do you mean by 'technology'?"

"You might have a portable TV, one of those fish-finders, a Blackberry—you know, that sort of thing."

Doris laughed loudly. "TV? The idea is to get away from the world! When I come out here, I leave the world on the shore. The way I look at, it doesn't do me any good to see 'em swimming under me on some monitor. Either the fish is on my hook, or it isn't. And the only use I got for a Blackberry is in a jam jar or on my peanut butter sandwich."

"But, you must have a radio?" Lou asked, assuming some connection to the outside world.

"I've got a weather radio that lets me know when a storm's coming."

"So, how long did it take you to make this hole, and where did the ice go?"

"Where did the ice go? Is that what you asked?" Doris asked. "Boy you *are* a city boy! Do I *really* have to answer that question?"

"The chopped ice goes outside, I take it."

"Well, it doesn't melt, I can't use it in here, and it doesn't sink. So yeah, outside is about my only option. I cut the section to the size I want it, and then I push the shanty over the hole."

"Okay. I didn't know whether you cut the hole after the shanty was in place or before. This rug keeps you from slipping into the drink, right?" Lou asked, pointing to the "floor."

"Hey, for a detective, you are one sharp fella," Doris replied, sounding a bit guilty for making fun of Lou.

"How do you get heat out here?"

"I bring it with me."

"Batteries?"

"For my flashlight, yeah, but I use propane gas for that heater over there," Doris said, pointing to a black box-like heater in one corner of the shanty.

"Are all of the shanties pretty much the same?"

"The insides are up to the imagination. You find pictures in some of them. Some have TVs with those DVDs so they can watch movies. Some have a case of beer and other potables. Most have brandy, because brandy is best for keeping your insides warm. You see, a fishing shanty is to a fisherman what a cabin is to a deer hunter. It's an escape. For some it isn't about catching fish, it's about being alone or with a good friend, having a drink. But for many, this is serious business. For them, the object in being out here is to feed their families. They don't mess around. They are year-round fishermen."

"I drove out here. I don't see a car for you. How do you get to and from shore?"

"I've got a quad."

"A quad?" Lou asked, seeking clarification.

"A small four-wheel-drive vehicle, big tires, you'll see them when you leave."

"Oh, I know what you mean. I didn't know they were called, 'quads.'"

"Well, you're out here to learn, and that's what you're doing."

"Where does the 'tip-up' come in?" Lou asked.

"They're outside. But if you don't look for them, you might miss them. They're orange devices, usually, and when the fish bites, it releases a spring and the flag flips up and you know you've got something, if only a bite."

"So, you fish, and every once in a while, you go out to monitor the tip-ups."

"You're catching on. Before you came out here, I saw a flag up. I took in a pike, but it was 23 inches, an inch short of the minimum length. So that one got another chance."

"I've got a strange question, Doris. Max may have told you I investigate murders. I'm wondering: Could you kill someone in a shanty?" Lou asked.

"Depends on how you plan to kill 'em," Doris replied. "Poisoning? Yeah, that could happen. Using a gun, yeah, bludgeoning a guy with an auger, yeah. If I were going to kill someone in here, I would want it silent and fast, so I'd probably use poison or garrote the guy."

"What would you do with the body?" Lou asked.

"What did I do with the ice? I chopped it up into pieces!" Doris replied, shaking her head. "You *sure* you're a detective?" Lou smiled, not taking the comment as a slam, but as a reference to his culture shock.

"What kind of fish do you catch out here?"

"Bluegill mostly, or pan fish.

"Well, thanks for the coffee. I told Max I'd only be a few minutes. I appreciate your hospitality, Doris. Good luck."

"Nice meeting you, Lou. Stop out anytime. You're always welcome in my home away from home."

"Many thanks. Here's my card, if you think of anything else you think I should know."

"Okay. You want more coffee for the road—er,—the ice?" Doris asked, proud of her humor.

"No thanks. I'm good to go." Lou opened the door and stepped from the warm interior into the frigid air where the wind chill was well below zero.

❋❋❋❋❋

Lou found Jack in the motel lounge where he was watching the big-screen TV broadcast of the Pistons vs. the Cleveland Cavaliers game. LeBron was having another big night, and the basketball seemed to have a magnet for the rim. As they cracked peanuts, the front desk manager approached. "Mr. Searing?"

"Yes."

"We received a call from someone named Buck, who said he had promised to get this for you." The manager handed Lou the note with George Zink's number.

"Thank you."

Lou watched another basket or two, then decided to call. He dialed the number on his cell.

"Hello," a woman's voice answered.

"Mrs. Zink?"

"Yes. Who's calling?"

"This is Lou Searing, calling from Houghton Lake. Is Mr. Zink available?"

"Just a minute." Lou heard the woman call, "George, it's for you."

"Who is it?" Lou heard from a distance.

"Somebody from Houghton Lake," she answered before the extension was picked up.

"Hello?"

"Mr. Zink?"

"Yes. Who am I talking to?"

"My name is Lou Searing. I'm looking into the disappearance of Harry Moody back in 1985. I understand you knew Harry, and that you are a good friend of Buck Brick. Could I ask you a few questions?"

"That was a long time ago—I probably don't remember much. Besides, I went into a serious depression after Harry disappeared."

"Are you better now?"

"Yes. Thanks to a loving wife and good therapy."

"I've been asked to solve this case," Lou began. "In doing so, your name came up as a friend of Harry's."

"Yes, we were friends."

"I realize it was twenty-five years ago, but do you remember him saying anything about coming into money?" Lou asked, hoping the question would fire some gray cells in George's brain.

"Well, first of all, you need to understand about Harry. He said whatever entered his mind. It made no difference that what he said should be kept quiet or might hurt him in the long run. Several times we, his friends, winced or shook our heads while he talked about someone or something going on in his life."

"I see," Lou replied.

"Now to your question. Yes, I recall him saying he would be coming into a lot of money; he mentioned it several times. Once when the two of us were together, he said, 'Guess you must be curious where I'm getting this pot of gold.' I said, 'Well, sure, we're all curious, but it isn't any of our business.'

"'I'll tell *you*, George,' he said, 'because I *like* you, and I *trust* you. But, don't tell anyone else, okay?' 'Okay,' I said, surprised to hear that he would actually say something to one of us and not to the others.

"'Insurance,' he said. 'I took out a big life insurance policy on my grandson, Todd—named myself the beneficiary. In the first place, his dad won't do that for him. Second, I'm sure Todd will die soon.'

"'Why should he die?'" I asked.

"'You can't be a pathological liar and live too long. He'll get himself into the wrong crowd, and then his lies will significantly hurt someone, and revenge will be the order of the day. So, when he dies, I'll get a lot of money, and you'll know why.' That was it—nothing more was ever said. The young man didn't die, but Harry did."

"Interesting," Lou remarked. "If Harry really was killed, who do you think is the murderer?"

"I don't know, or I would have said so. But, if I had to guess, just a gut feeling, I'd have to say his son, Junior, did his dad in."

"Because?" Lou asked.

"Because he hated Harry. No one else *hated* Harry, at least, no one I know of. But he and Junior got into shouting matches whenever they were in each other's presence. It was devastating to Todd. They didn't protect him. In fact, each of them wanted Todd to see how strong he was."

"If Junior *didn't* kill his father, who is your second suspect?" Lou asked.

"Todd."

"Really?" Lou asked surprised. "Why?"

"Killing Harry would end the conflict between his dad and grandfather. One thing not many people realize is that Todd never lied to Harry. When Harry caught him lying to him once, he literally beat him. He said he did it to teach Todd a lesson. Apparently it worked, because the beating seemed to cure him."

"I hadn't heard about that incident. But I've been going on the assumption that Harry was murdered. Do you think he simply left town on his own?"

"Not a chance. Harry was a 'routine' guy. He couldn't handle change."

"Could someone have kidnapped him?"

"If you're thinking Junior or Todd, yes, that could have happened. If you mean anyone else, no, I don't think he was kidnapped."

"Those are my questions. Thanks for talking with me," Lou said.

"Hope I helped," George said. "Good luck. I'm one of many who'd like to have it finally explained."

Lou reported the conversation to Jack, and then called Carol.

"I was just getting ready to call you," Carol said sounding relieved. "Apparently someone tried to break into our house this afternoon."

"Did they get in?" Lou asked, naturally concerned.

"No; our neighbors heard Samm barking and looked across at our place. Janice saw someone trying to lift our dining room windows. Dick knew that you were gone and I was at church, so he called the police, who came right out. They found no point of entry or broken windows, no crowbar marks."

"That's something to be thankful for, I guess," Lou said.

"I don't mean to be a wimp, but I'm staying at Scott and Patti's tonight. If I am alone, every sound I hear would be my imagination telling me someone is outside waiting."

"That's a good idea. Did Janice say whether the person was a man or a woman, young or old?"

"She thought the prowler was in his forties. The person got into a motor home and drove away before the police arrived."

"Did the police find any footprints in the snow around the house?" Lou asked hoping they had investigated carefully.

"Oh yes, they took notes and photos, measured footprints, got fingerprints off the windows. They were meticulous. They were at the Searing home, and they wouldn't do an investigation that was less than thorough."

"And this was in broad daylight?" Lou asked.

"Yes, about three o'clock this afternoon."

"It doesn't sound like an attempted break-in," Lou said. "Perhaps someone was simply trying to see if anybody was home, and he was a bit more thorough than ringing the doorbell."

"You may be right, but I'm still going to spend the night in Grand Rapids."

"Good plan. I'll be home tomorrow. Love you."

"Do you think this is related to your cold case?" Carol asked.

"Maybe, but I doubt it."

Carol had no more than ended her conversation with Lou when the phone rang again. The caller introduced himself as Tom Babcock and began to apologize. "Mrs. Searing, I am sorry to have caused concern this afternoon. We're touring the country in our mobile home, stopping occasionally to visit friends. Unfortunately, I took down our friends' address and wrote a 'one' instead of a 'seven.' So, when we stopped this afternoon, we thought we were at our friends' house. They were not expecting us, but we thought they would be home, and when no one answered the door, we walked around and knocked on the windows. They too have a dog, so when your dog barked we just assumed it was our friends' dog."

"That's good to hear. Our neighbors told us someone was trying to break into our house."

"Yes, and they called the police. We have also called the police and explained our behavior."

"So, if you confused the 'seven' for a 'one'—you must be friends of the Parkers?"

"Yes, we're the Babcocks, Tom and Cindy. We went to Boston College together. By the way, they are quite embarrassed also. Peggy Parker will be contacting you soon."

"Please tell Peggy that isn't necessary. Mistakes happen. Thanks so much for calling, because it puts my mind at ease."

"You're welcome, and again, I'm sorry for giving you a scare today."

Carol relaxed. "Say 'hi' to Hugh and Peggy for me, and enjoy your visit."

Carol called Lou and shared the mistake that caused the neighbors to call the police. He was happy to hear that the episode could be explained.

JANUARY 19

Jack and Lou rose, prepared for check-out, ate their complimentary breakfast and headed to the parking lot. Lou scraped the snow and ice off of his car windows while Jack put their luggage in the trunk. The car had been idling to heat it a bit and make sure the windshield was clear for safe driving. With a notebook of information, Lou and Jack headed back to west Michigan.

Over the next three days, Lou made several calls in an attempt to find someone who knew Harry's wife well. The only name he could come up with was a neighbor, Dianna Lutz. Max knew that Dianna was good friends with Estelle Moody, and he seemed confident that Dianna would recall Harry's disappearance.

Lou called Dianna and explained the purpose of his call.

"Yes, Mr. Searing, I saw the article in the Resorter and gave some thought to going to the motel to talk to you. But I decided that anything I would say, you had probably already heard, and I was reluctant to get involved."

"All information is good, even what we've heard before. No two people have the same memory, or one person will add something to give us a different slant on the facts."

"How can I help you?"

"I'm curious about Mrs. Moody's reaction to Harry's disappearance. Did she mention anything that Harry might have said prior to his leaving that afternoon? I also wonder whether she had any idea who might have killed him, if in fact, she believed he was murdered. I understand you were a good friend so I assume that if she were going to share feelings or ideas with anyone, it would be you."

"You've asked several questions. I didn't write each down, so if you would repeat each one, I'll do my best to answer."

"Okay. Did Estelle Moody have any thoughts about Harry's disappearance?"

"Well, I remember that she was in denial. She was convinced Harry would call any minute, or walk in the door any second. Both his truck and his snowmobile were outside the house. Estelle was worried, concerned, she kept to herself. She didn't have many visitors—I think people felt uncomfortable talking to her during that time.

"After about a week, she began to accept that he was not coming home—that something had happened to him. Now that I think about it, I recall her saying Harry told her he was going to visit some friends who lived near Dead Stream Swamp."

"I have not heard about this Dead Stream Swamp. Where is that?" Lou asked.

"It's on the west side of the four-lane highway, a very marshy area near the Muskegon River, sort of connected with the Riverdale Dam. Hunters go into that area looking for deer, and, so the stories go, a few of them don't come out."

"Did she think Harry had been murdered?" Lou asked. "If so, did she have any idea who might have killed him?"

"As I said, at first she was in denial, and then she accepted he was not coming home, but she never mentioned the word 'murder.' She thought he got lost in Dead Stream Swamp. Maybe he got disoriented in the swamp during a whiteout and fell and struck his head on something. But the one thing she could not understand was why his snowmobile was at the house. She asked me over and over, 'How could his snowmobile be here, but not him?' That bothered her for weeks."

"So, Estelle never thought Harry was murdered?" Lou asked.

"It was a process, denial and then acceptance, but without a thought of murder. Eventually she talked about that possibility, but she never said anything like, 'I think so-and-so murdered Harry.' She knew there was no love lost between Junior and Harry. Very sad, Mr. Searing."

"How did she get along with Junior?" Lou asked.

"Junior was a 'mama's boy.' He could do no wrong, so their relationship was a good one."

"Did Junior comfort his mother after his father disappeared?" Lou asked.

"He'd call or drop by once in a while, but he didn't seem too concerned because he thought Estelle was adjusting well."

"Did Junior mourn his father's death?" Lou asked.

"Not as far as I could tell. There was a memorial service a month or so after Harry disappeared, and as I recall, Junior didn't attend. People talked about that, believe me!"

"How about Todd Moody. Was he there?"

"Yes. He sat with his grandmother and seemed to grieve. In fact, he spoke during the time when people share thoughts or memories."

"Do you know who Harry would have visited in the Dead Stream Swamp?" Lou asked.

"More than likely it would have been Rich and Paula Doucette. Nice folks. He knew Rich from fishing and hunting. They would play cards and drink at the Nottingham Bar."

"Where is that?" Lou asked.

"Where M-55 and old U.S. 27 meet—right near the state police post."

"I certainly appreciate you sharing your recollections, Mrs. Lutz. Please get in touch if you remember anything else."

"I will. Glad I could help, Mr. Searing"

JANUARY 24

Lou and Jack needed to put their heads together. They met at the K.P. Galley Restaurant in Spring Lake to formulate a theory about what might have happened to Harry on January 17, 1985. Coffee and bagels made room for notebooks and laptops as they began to share ideas.

"So, Mr. Kelly, do you see any patterns?" Lou asked.

"You know me, I always have a theory. My problem is I don't always have facts to support it."

"Well, let's hear it. I'm curious what you've come up with."

"Harry was murdered," Jack began. "The killer left Harry's wallet in the woods to give authorities the impression Harry was hiking or hunting, got lost, and dropped his wallet, hoping someone would find it and keep looking for him. Since no body was ever found, Harry's bones are either in Dead Stream Swamp or at the bottom of Houghton Lake. Now, who killed him or why, I don't know yet."

"I agree with you," Lou replied. "I'd add that the killer returned Harry's snowmobile to his home, but he apparently didn't know enough to put the tarp back over it. If we believe Lawrence, that Harry only took his snowmobile when he went ice fishing, Harry went to the lake, or at least in that direction."

"He had a shanty, and he has friends in shanties," Jack said. "So we can conclude he was going to his shanty, the shanty of a friend, or to someone else's fishing spot."

"Makes sense," Lou replied. "Normally he would go to his own shanty, but there was no sign of his being there, nor of a struggle—no evidence of any kind, according to the police report. I'm inclined to think he went to a friend's shanty."

"Or, he was lured to a shanty belonging to a stranger, or to someone who was not a friend."

"Could have happened," Lou conceded.

"Did we get DNA from that White Sox cap?" Jack asked.

"There's no report yet. But, if it's Harry's DNA on that cap, it means that he didn't go ice fishing," Lou concluded. "Again, I'm hanging my theory on Lawrence's comments. And I'm afraid that Sox cap is the only lead we have."

"We might ask Estelle Moody if we could look at anything of Harry's she has left, now that twenty-five years have passed," Jack suggested.

"Let me think about that one," Lou replied. "You know, people have routines, but sometimes they step out of routine because of a lapse of memory, or convenience or any number of reasons. Harry could have started out wearing the hat heading to his shanty, and the wind could have carried it away and 'hidden' it until spring."

"Nobody has mentioned the possibility of suicide," Jack said. "Maybe Harry simply jumped into the lake through the hole in his shanty. His cap came off and floated to the surface in the spring thaw, and his bones are still down there."

"We need to look at all possibilities, but there's no indication that he was depressed or in any trouble to warrant such drastic action," Lou replied. "Let's put that suggestion to rest."

"Just covering all the bases," Jack replied.

"I'm intrigued by the notion that Harry's bones could be on the bottom of Houghton Lake. It's possible, just as it's possible they're in Dead Stream Swamp." Lou's face brightened.

"Or, his body could be seated in a bar in Jackson Hole, Wyoming." Jack guffawed.

Lou's cell phone rang as the two were about to leave the restaurant.

"Is this Mr. Searing?"

"Yes. Who's calling?"

"This is Josh Higbee from Houghton Lake."

"Yes, Mr. Higbee."

"I felt guilty rebuffing you when you called a while back. The more I thought about it, the more I knew I should have helped you. Max gave me your number. I hope you don't mind."

"No, I'm glad you called."

"You wanted to talk about Junior Moody. Someone told you we were friends?"

"Yes, that was the purpose of my call."

"Well, he was a tortured man, Mr. Searing. If ever a guy was not where he needed to be, it was Junior Moody. He was a square peg living in a world of round holes. He was a good friend to me, but he hated his father. Harry was always putting Junior down, ridiculing him, and doing it in front of Junior's son."

"That's sad."

"Yeah, it tore Junior up. He was just the opposite of his father. Junior dressed neatly, was clean-shaven, went to church, had a good job, kept his house in good condition. We played poker with a group of guys every Wednesday evening at his house."

"Did he talk about his father?"

"No, home was one place he didn't have to face his father."

"I see. I don't know how to soften my question, so I'll ask it outright. Do you think Junior could have killed his father?"

"Absolutely not. Junior was a God-fearing man. He lived by the Ten Commandments."

"I try not to judge, Josh, but are you sure he honored his father?"

"He honored Harry, but he had to defend himself against him. At least that's how I saw it."

"How about Todd Moody—could he have killed his grand-father?"

"I doubt it. Poor boy, he was so torn between these two men fighting for his love and respect. If anything, I can see

Todd killing *himself* to escape, but as I knew the kid, even if he thought about it, murder was not in him."

"As I understand it, Junior's wife is still living."

"That's correct. Her name is Sherri."

"And, as far as you know, Junior didn't admit or seek forgiveness on his deathbed for killing Harry."

"I never heard, but I wasn't near where he died—down south someplace, Mississippi, or Alabama."

"Thank you, Mr. Higbee. I appreciate the call. Your insights are helpful."

"You're welcome. Will you let me know what you learn once you conclude the investigation?"

"Yes, I definitely will."

"A lot of people think Junior killed his dad, so it would please me if and when Junior is exonerated."

"Thanks for calling, Mr. Higbee."

Jack had waited patiently while Lou hurriedly wrote in his notebook. Lou summarized: "Mr. Higbee is sure that neither Junior nor Todd killed Harry. That's it in a nutshell, but I give him credit for changing his mind about calling us."

CHAPTER
SIX

The Tip-Up Town Festival would be celebrated over the next two weekends. Lou figured there was no sense in inviting Carol to go along; the freezing temperatures involved were enough to put an end to that discussion. But, to be courteous, he did ask if she wanted to go to the winter festival—and he got a quick and immediate answer: "You have to be kidding!"

Lou hedged, "Well, yes, I guess, but I wanted you to feel welcome to come."

"I'll stay here by the fireplace with Samm and Millie. You go and have a good time."

"You know I'm not going to have 'a good time.' I'm going to work on the Moody case."

"Is Jack going?" Carol asked.

"I'll ask him to go. If he is available, I'm sure he will."

"I'll think of you while I have my hot tea. Call me if I miss anything."

Jack quickly agreed to join Lou. Since all the festival-area motels had been booked for months, Lou suggested an early start on a one-day visit to Houghton Lake. Fortunately, the sky was blue and no snow was forecast, but it was bitter cold and the wind chill made the layering of winter wear essential.

Lou and Jack arrived in mid-morning, and as luck would have it, a car pulled out of a prime spot as close to Tip-Up Town as one could get. All Tip-Up Town activities take place on or very near the water's edge, or in this season, the shore of the frozen lake. Tip-Up Town resembles a town even more in that participants elect a mayor and other "city" officials.

A huge poster advertising the Polar Bear Dip was the first sign of an event they encountered. Lou couldn't understand what he was seeing. "There is no way sane human beings would jump into that water with only a swim suit to protect them from the ice-cold water."

"The purpose of the suit is to cover the privates, Lou," Jack said. "People actually find the cold dip invigorating."

"People who do this should take an IQ test," Lou said. "That score needs to equal the water temperature for someone even to consider doing such a thing."

"Let's watch it. It takes place later in the day," Jack suggested. "You might change your mind."

"We'll watch it, but I won't change my mind."

"I checked out the Tip-Up Town web site and they have some videos of last year's activities," Jack replied. "Participants jump in with a good-sized rope around their waist."

"Rope?" Lou asked.

"Well, yeah. If there is a problem, the body needs to get out, and nobody is going to jump in to rescue the participant."

"Okay, then they get out?" Lou stated the obvious.

"Yes, but they have to swim about ten feet to a ladder to climb out."

"Swim?" Lou asked, dumbfounded. "It's not enough just to get wet, they have to swim, too?"

"It's all part of the event." Jack grinned at Lou's incredulous expression.

"This is only for overweight people, right?" Lou asked. "I mean, you need blubber to protect your organs from the shock of that sudden drop in temperature, don't you?"

"The ones I saw aren't overweight. They're just normal-looking people."

"To each his own, I guess." Lou still couldn't imagine the event.

"I think the body adjusts to the conditions," Jack said, trying to help Lou understand. "They're in and out in a matter of seconds, and then they put on protective clothing and get into a warm environment. Want to try it Lou?"

"Is the Pope Methodist?" Lou asked. "You've got to be out of your ever-loving mind," Lou blustered. "It's all I can do to stand on the ice wearing seven layers of clothes!" Jack laughed, and so did Lou.

"You're always looking for an interesting experience. I just assumed you'd give it a try."

"Well, you assumed wrong, Jack. Now, frozen turkey bowling, that sounds like fun. I'll enter that."

"I thought we came here to do some serious detecting, Lou."

"We did, but I'm caught up in some of the activities. They have fishing contests, too, I hope."

"I'm sure they do. Probably for the most fish caught, or the biggest," Jack replied.

"I think catching walleye in winter is illegal, but pan fish and bluegill are fair game."

"Back to the case, Lou," Jack said, becoming serious. "What are the plans for today?"

"First, I want to attend this festival. Since our incident took place here 25 years ago, I want to experience it, to see if anything comes to mind."

"What do you want me to do?" Jack asked.

"Get yourself invited into one of the shanties, talk to the fishermen, survey the area," Lou suggested. "Oh, and when you pick a shanty, avoid those pop-up fabric coverings they use today. Choose a shanty that looks like it could have been used twenty-five years ago."

"You think I can just walk up, knock on the door, and be invited in?" Jack asked.

"I don't see why not. You might talk to some of the fishermen outside the shanties and ask who might welcome a visitor."

"That's a good idea. Okay, I'm heading on to Tip-Up Town. If I need you, I'll call on the cell. We can meet at the Welcome Center in two hours, unless one of us needs more time."

❄❄❄❄❄

As Jack headed out to meet fishermen and visit a shanty, Lou decided to go up in a single-engine plane to observe the festivities from high over Houghton Lake. He drove west to the Houghton Lake Airport where rides were being offered, paid his fee, and waited for his turn to take to the air. His pilot was Luke Slayton, a man of about 30.

"Any particular place you want to fly, Lou?"

"I'd like to fly over the festival area a few times. And I'd like to see Dead Stream Swamp. I would also like to look down on St. Helen. That's about it, I guess."

"You by yourself?" Luke asked.

"Yes, I am."

"Do you mind if we take a couple of folks with us?"

"Not at all, but I'd like the seat next to you, because I might have some questions."

"I'm okay with that. Let me get a couple of folks for the back seats."

In a matter of a few minutes, Luke returned and introduced Lou to a father and daughter, Tim and Tonya Tyler. The four climbed into the plane, buckled in, and listened carefully to Luke's pre-flight instructions.

As the plane took off into the west wind, Lou looked down on U.S. 27, the stretch of four-lane highway which, along with I-75, makes up the north-to-south mid-Michigan travel route. To the north he saw Higgins Lake, a sister lake to Houghton, separated by a few miles of swampland. The Muskegon River swirled like a string from a balloon around to the northwest; it would ultimately flow into Lake Michigan, a hundred and twenty miles west of Houghton Lake.

Luke got Lou's attention over the sound of the engine, and shouted, "You wanted to see Dead Stream Swamp—it's the stretch of land from your right to my left. I'll go north, then turn to the south, and you'll see the whole area as you look out your window." Luke turned toward his back-seat passengers and shouted, "When I head south, you can see Tip-Up Town on the left and Dead Stream Swamp on the right."

Lou wasn't sure what he expected to see, but he wanted to know where the swamp was and what the terrain was like. As they approached the swamp, Luke said to Lou, "Hunters have gone into that area and never come out."

"Doesn't look large enough that someone wouldn't come out," Lou replied.

"When you factor in snow, ice, and freezing temperatures, once you get disoriented, the swamp is large enough to simply swallow you."

"I take it you can walk in there?" Lou asked.

"Hunters go in there, but you need to know where you're going. Depending on the season, rainfall, river current, and ground condition, it can be a perfect place for deer hunting—or a death-trap."

The small plane, now flying due south, banked to the east after it passed M-55, the east-west primary road. Luke made a couple of passes over Tip-Up Town and St. Helen. From their place in the sky, the passengers could see shanties on the lake, ice fishermen, the festival activities, and thousands of people trying to stay warm while enjoying Michigan's most popular winter festival.

After the fifteen-minute ride, Luke landed at the airport and tied the plane down. As the four walked back to the small building which served as office and hangar, Tim Tyler said something that struck Lou: "You know, if I found a good fishing spot for my shanty, I would want to GPS the spot, so I could set up there next year." Tonya, his daughter didn't understand, but Lou and Luke thought the suggestion a good one.

"Is that possible?" Lou asked.

"Oh, sure. It's a stretch to think a good fishing spot this year will be as good next year, but if someone wanted to be in the same spot, it's definitely easy to mark it."

✳✳✳✳✳

While Lou flew over Tip-Up Town, Jack approached a man sitting on a stool by a nine-inch-wide hole monitoring a tip-up signal device. Jack asked him if he knew a friendly guy he could talk to about ice fishing in a shanty. The fellow pointed to his right and replied, "Go talk to Craig Allen. He's a story-teller, and a good fisherman. In fact, I'll call him on his cell and tell him you're on your way."

"Thanks! Good fishing to you!"

A few minutes later Jack knocked on the door, entered, and said, "Craig? Thanks for sharing your shanty." He offered his hand, "Jack Kelly."

"Yeah, I'm Craig. Welcome to my home. I've got coffee on the heater and a seat for you."

"Thanks. I don't want to be in your way," Jack replied. "Shall I sit on this bench? And, thanks for the offer of coffee. That'd be great." The bench was hard but comfortable.

As Craig poured coffee into a cup, he said, "Thanks for the company. It gets kind of lonely out here, especially when they aren't biting. Part of being out here is to get away from the noisy, chaotic world, but an occasional visitor is welcome. What do you want to know?"

"I'm working with Lou Searing on a cold case."

"Well, you're sure in the right place to work on a cold case," Craig said with a smile.

"Yes, and this one is really frozen in time. How is that for an analogy?" Jack asked.

"Pretty good. What's your cold case?" Craig asked.

"The unexplained disappearance of Harry Moody back in 1985," Jack replied.

"You'll never solve that one," Craig said with assurance. "That one will be cold till hell freezes over, Jack."

"Why do you say that?"

"Just about everybody figures he was probably kidnapped and taken somewhere and killed."

"That's the general theory, huh?"

"Yeah, pretty much. Folks think whoever kidnapped Harry tossed his wallet into the woods to give the impression he got lost in a whiteout. But maybe Harry was hoping someone would find it, and then eventually find him. The kidnappers knew a lot about Harry including his boast that he was coming into money. Someone took his snowmobile home to make people believe that he went home that night. They probably knocked him out somehow, and whoever kidnapped him, drove a long ways away. They collected the money he supposedly had stashed, and then killed him."

"That makes sense," Jack replied.

"Yeah, a lot of us think that's what happened to Harry. And, the cops never found any skeleton, clothes, anything to indicate he was still around here. It's a waste of your time, Jack.

But I suppose you like solving murders as much as I like fishing, so, to each his own."

"Mind if I ask you a few questions?"

"Go right ahead. I haven't had a bite in more than an hour. Just understand that if I do, my attention is going to my dinner."

"That's a given."

"Question number one?" Craig asked.

"Let's say the killer was a fisherman in a shanty, like you," Jack began. "How would you carry out the murder?" he asked.

"It would have to be quiet and fast. Quiet, because I wouldn't want anyone hearing shouting or banging around in this small wooden room. Fast—again, my first answer, because I wouldn't want any noise or struggle."

"That makes sense. So, how would you kill a man?" Jack asked.

"Well, I haven't had much experience," Craig said with a chuckle. "I mean, zero experience, thankfully. But I guess if I were going to do it, it would have to be poisoning—or maybe garroting the guy."

"Okay, let's say you garrote him. How do you keep him from falling in the hole?"

"If I were going to do it in here, I'd put a wooden cover over the hole. 'Cause, when he dropped down, he'd need that space to lie on."

"Okay, now we've a man dead on the floor. The killing was fast and made no noise. Now what do you do?" Jack asked.

"That's a problem. I'd have to carry a fully-clothed dead weight out of here, and then I've got a 'people' problem— I couldn't get out of here without people seeing and questioning me. Saying he's a passed-out drunk wouldn't work because Harry was known by most fisherman out here, most local fishermen, anyway."

"So, do you leave him here overnight?"

"Nope—I'd have the same problem the next day."

"Right. So what do you do?"

"I guess I would flush him down the toilet. Down the hole that is."

"Exactly. But, a fully-clothed body might float. Right?"

"Or it might sink," Craig mused. "Wet boots, heavy coat, and leggings just might be enough to make the body go down."

"So, if you wanted to make sure the body would sink, what would you do?" Jack asked.

"Weight it, I guess."

"How?"

"A few boat anchors would do the trick," Craig replied.

"You don't want any clothing coming to the surface," Jack hypothesized. "So, do you remove the clothes and take them with you off the lake?"

"I guess that would work, but seems like you want this to happen quickly. You can't predict when another fisherman will knock on your door to chat and find some warmth. I guess I'd get some rope or duct tape and wrap it tightly around the legs, arms and torso."

"Okay. Then once clothes are taped to the body and boat anchors tied to both arms and legs, you just remove the wooden covering over the hole, and down he goes?"

"Yeah, I suppose that would work."

"No body, no blood, no fingerprints, no witnesses—Harry just disappears. You drive his snowmobile back to his home, park it, and leave. Done!" Jack summarized.

"Hey, you're pretty good. That's what you think happened?" Craig asked.

"I'm not sure, but the scenario makes sense, doesn't it?"

"I guess so." Just then, Craig's bobber sank, and he grabbed his pole and began reeling it in. Jack watched the drama, wondering if a whale would appear. It wasn't a whale, but a good-sized pike.

"Looks like you just caught your dinner," Jack said.

"I'll call the Missus and tell her I'm 'bringing home the bacon.' She'll understand."

"Thanks for talking with me, Mr. Allen."

"I hope I helped."

"You did. We talked through one possibility that would explain Harry's disappearance. I appreciate your hospitality." Jack shook Craig's hand, then left the warm shanty and carefully ventured over the ice.

❄❄❄❄❄

Meeting at Booners, a local restaurant, to share experiences above and on the ice, Jack urged Lou, "They're about to start the Polar Bear Dip! Come on, let's check it out!" The two men walked to where they saw a rectangle of open water that was perhaps 20 by 15 feet. The announcer was explaining to participants and observers what was about to happen.

Five women, shivering in thick robes stood with other soon-to-be-wet participants. Lou approached the group. "Excuse me, it's none of my business, but do you realize what you're about to do? And if you do, why on God's good earth would you think about doing such a ridiculous thing?"

Cindy Collins smiled patiently and said, "We're the Crazy Ladies from Laingsburg. We do this every year."

"So, you really do know what to expect?" Lou asked, shaking his head.

"Oh, yes. We collect pledges back home and give the money to our local food bank and other charities," Dale Joan Collins said.

"How much do you raise?" Jack asked.

"Well, we raise a minimum of two thousand dollars for each of us to jump in," replied Heather Joy Spotts.

"And people give you money believing you'll actually jump into this frozen pond?"

"See that man over there with the video camera, the one with the red cap?" said Connie Spotts.

"Yes."

"He's Mel Spotts, my dad. He takes a video and then puts it together with music. We show it to civic and church groups back home. That way, we have proof we really did jump in and swim at Tip-Up Town."

"Well, your name is perfect, 'The Crazy Ladies of Laingsburg!' Will you introduce us to the other freezing women?"

Cindy motioned to the three others. "These are Crazy Theresa Driscoll, Crazy Lin Reed, and Crazy Pat Spitzley." The three women smiled tightly and offered a chilly "Pleased to meet you."

"Then I should say, 'Congratulations,' because you are supporting good causes. Enjoy your dip!" Lou waved as he walked away.

Lou said to Jack quietly as they joined the crowd. "Seems like a bake sale would be a lot easier."

"Yes, but you gotta hand it to them. They take life by the horns and live each day to the hilt."

The Crazy Ladies of Laingsburg did their thing. Each woman jumped into the freezing water, surfaced, and swam to the ladder. Lou just shook his head in disbelief. "Let's get warm," Jack said.

On the way back to the car, Lou noticed the frozen turkey bowling competition. Getting into the spirit of the festival, Lou said, "I think I can put those pins down with a Butterball."

Jack guffawed. "I'd rather watch you splash into that pond with the Crazy Ladies! But bowling is better than nothing, I suppose."

Lou paid the fee, chose the roundest bird, took a few steps, and let her fly, figuratively speaking. The frozen turkey bumped along and—even though Lou hit the 1-3 pocket—stopped in the middle of the pins for a total score of six.

"Not bad, my friend," Jack shouted from the sideline.

"At least I didn't butter the turkey," Lou said.

"Gutter, you mean you didn't gutter the turkey."

"Whatever," Lou grinned as the two headed for the Family Tent and a cup of hot chocolate.

After discussing the day's experiences and their flight and shanty conversations, they decided to head home. They had no immediate leads to follow, no one new to interview, and no particular place to visit. It had been a long day. Three hours later Lou and Jack pulled into their respective driveways, both thankful to be home and warm.

❄❄❄❄❄

Carol greeted Lou with a hug and kiss. As Lou unbuttoned his heavy coat, Carol said, "Oh, how I miss our walks along the lake shore. Samm, you, and I can simply let the world go by while we walk and share what's on our minds."

"I miss them, too, but it's only a few months until we can enjoy warm sand and water lapping up and over our feet and ankles. Meanwhile, we can remember and dream."

"Since we can't walk on the beach, let's sit in front of the fire. I'll get you some Mackinaw Island Fudge ice cream, and then I want to hear about your day at the festival. After you left, I thought perhaps I should have gone to offer you moral support."

Lou hung up his heavy coat and took off his boots. "Thanks, but I think I'll pass on the ice cream; I've had enough cold for the day. I'll take a cup of tea, though. It wasn't necessary that you go, but thanks for the thought. I've not much to tell, really. We drove over there. I went for a plane ride to get a better idea of the terrain. Jack interviewed a fisherman in a shanty and got some good ideas. We met the Five Crazy Ladies from Laingsburg who raise money for charity by jumping into the water at the Polar Bear Dip—they were crazy, all right. And, I knocked down six pins in the frozen turkey bowling event."

"Did you win a kewpie doll?" Carol asked.

"No. I didn't win a thing, but I added a few dollars to the festival coffers. That, plus lunch and a hot chocolate."

❄❄❄❄❄

Sitting in front of the fire with feet up on ottomans and Samm and Millie lying by their chairs, Lou and Carol took deep breaths and began to relax.

"So, what did you do today?" Lou asked.

"I went shopping. We have a couple of January birthdays on the calendar, and I wanted to get gifts and have them mailed. I also stopped in to see the travel agent."

"Hummm, where are we going now?" Lou asked, realizing he might soon be in France, or Norway, or Italy.

"I picked up brochures about cruises in France. And I saw one I especially thought you might like, along the coast of Norway. It goes north of the Arctic Circle."

"Sounds fine to me. When are you thinking about going?"

"Summer or early fall, as usual." She paused glancing at Lou. "Are you and Jack closer to wrapping up this case?"

"Not much. We're still in the fact-gathering stage, but we've come up with some theories."

"Like what?"

"Harry was killed in an ice shanty and then stuffed down the fishing hole."

"You're kidding!" Carol said, aghast.

"Nope, not kidding. Anything is possible."

"That would give new meaning to the Polar Bear Dip," Carol said, with a hint of a chuckle.

"Harry just disappeared. He was kidnapped, eaten by a bear, or flushed. No bones or clothing were found. Well, actually there's a baseball cap, but we don't know whether it belonged to Harry."

"You'll solve the mystery. You always do."

"Remember the night of the snowstorm, when that couple visited us?" Lou asked.

"Yes. That started this whole thing."

"Right. Well, that man, Todd, is a pathological liar. It is nerve-wracking, because we can't believe a word he says."

"Is he related to Harry?"

"Yes, we're sure of that. But otherwise, all we can trust is information we get from locals who know or knew Todd. We assume they're telling the truth. But they could be repeating Todd's lies thinking they are true."

"That's weird."

"Par for the course. I've never run into a pathological liar, so it's a new experience."

"I'm sure you want to check your e-mail," Carol said. "I'll stay here and watch TV."

Lou went upstairs to his office and turned on his computer. An e-mail from Jack with a subject of, "Cold Case Closed," roused his curiosity.

Jack's e-mail read: "This case is closed, Lou. Give me a call when you get a minute, and I'll explain. I didn't call, because I figured you were spending time with Carol in front of a fire or something, and you wouldn't want to be disturbed. It was a lot of wasted time on our part, but I always enjoy working with and learning from you."

Immediately, Lou picked up his cell and called Jack. "What's this all about, partner?"

Well, when I got home, I received an e-mail from Jim Fordyce of LansingTalk.net. Jim did a piece on our opening of the Moody case. Soon thereafter he got an e-mail from an internet listener in Idaho who said a Harry Moody, formerly of Michigan, had died recently near Boise. Jim thought we should know, so he forwarded the e-mail to me."

"Okay, but there are probably hundreds of Harry Moodys, living and dead, throughout the country."

"I really think this is our Harry Moody. The obit is dated November 30. 'Harold [Harry] Moody, mountain man and local hermit, has died. About twenty-five years ago Mr. Moody came to our community from Michigan.' The 'community' they're talking about is Orchard, in Ada County, Idaho. Back to the obit. 'He had no family, and the officials have found no next of kin. Mr. Moody carried no wallet, so identification was made from letters addressed to him. He occasionally lived as a homeless man, but he spent most of his time in a small cabin he claimed many years ago. Mr. Moody will be buried in a community burial plot unless a relative can be found and confirmed.

Rumor has it he gained a fortune while in Michigan, but friends from the homeless shelter think his boasts were all talk.'"

"That's a strange obit," Lou admitted. "But, those small-town writers have a way of getting right to the point. It does sound like our Harry, but you know me, Jack—it isn't enough for me. I'm going to contact Todd and invite him to fly out to Idaho with me. We'll see if photos of the Idaho Moody are available, or if Todd recognizes any belongings they might have stored. You want to come along?"

"No thanks, Lou. January in Idaho holds about the same fascination for me that the Polar Bear Dip holds for you. Just let me know what you find."

Todd Moody did want to go to Idaho with Lou. He would meet Lou at Gerald R. Ford International Airport. After calling a travel agent to make flight arrangements, Lou called the Sheriff in Ada County, Idaho.

"Sheriff, this is Lou Searing, a private investigator in Michigan. I'm working on a case from 1985 involving a man named Harry Moody."

"I'm Sheriff Ron Bingham. How can I help you?"

"My investigative partner, Jack Kelly, has learned of an obituary for a Harold Moody who died a couple of months ago in Orchard."

"We handled that death, but we found nothing suspicious."

"Is the body buried yet?" Lou asked.

"No, we're waiting for a common burial for indigents."

"If I flew out there with a relative of Mr. Moody's, could we view the body?"

"As long as it isn't claimed before then by someone with a legal right to it," Ron replied.

"Did the coroner get a tissue sample for DNA, or take fingerprints or dental impressions?"

"No, we had no reason to do any of that. The Medical Examiner said it was a heart attack. We found no evidence of foul play, just a dead hermit who had a heart attack. He owned practically nothing and didn't owe a penny. He had no will, probably because he didn't have assets to disperse. But, sure, you're welcome to come out with the relative. We'll give you whatever information we have."

"Is his cabin still standing? Was it locked when he died? Has the place been cleared out?"

"Yes, yes, and no."

"I'd like to see what's in his cabin," Lou said. "Your Harold Moody might be my Harry Moody, and then again, they could be different men."

"Let me know when you'll arrive. A deputy will meet you at the airport and bring you and the relative to my office. You can view the body, and we can answer your questions and let you into the cabin. With luck, all of that will help with your case."

"Thanks, Sheriff Bingham."

"Let me know when you plan to be here."

"Will do, and thanks!"

✳✳✳✳✳

JANUARY 28

Lou and Todd flew from Grand Rapids to Minneapolis, changed planes to Denver, and then boarded a third flight to Boise. An Ada County sheriff's deputy met them at the airport and drove them to the sheriff's office in Orchard, twenty-five miles southeast. Sheriff Bingham had hot coffee ready and a file folder containing specifics of Harold Moody's death on his desk.

Introductions were made and the men talked about their flights and discussed whether Lou or Todd had been in Idaho before. Todd said he had been there as a child. Although the sheriff accepted Todd's comment, Lou was skeptical and now automatically assumed that whatever Todd said was false.

"I have put everything about Harold in this folder," Sheriff Bingham said. "You'll find the obituary, an article on homeless people that was published in the local paper a couple of years ago, a few photos, and a series of articles about homelessness. Harry is quoted quite often in those articles. You can study them, and I'll make copies if you want to take any with you."

"Thank you," Lou replied. "I appreciate your doing this."

"Not a problem. Now, you wanted to view the body, and if I recall correctly, you want to look around his cabin, right?"

"That's right."

"Why don't you finish your coffee while it's hot and review what's in the folder," Sheriff Bingham suggested. "Then we'll drive to the county morgue. You can then check out the cabin, and we'll get you back to Boise for your flight home."

"Sounds like a plan," Lou said, grateful for the efficient itinerary.

"Now, I have an errand at the court house," Sheriff Bingham said, rising. "When I get back, we'll go to the morgue."

Lou and Todd looked over the written material and photos. As far as they could tell, it seemed possible that Harry Moody had indeed traveled far from Tip-Up Town.

Lou showed Todd a photo. "Is this your grandfather?"

"I haven't seen him in 25 years, but it looks like him."

Lou had no idea. The man in the photo had an untrimmed beard and moustache and a full head of gray hair under a ragged Denver Broncos cap. Lou re-read the obituary Jack had received from an internet radio listener. Next he read the article on homelessness. Another photo showed Harry sitting under a bridge which he called 'home.' The material offered no clue to any other identity of 'Harry Moody.'

Whatever Todd looked at elicited the same response: "This is Gramps, alright. These quotes sound like him. Here, see where he says, 'You betcha'?" Todd asked. "That was a common phrase with Gramps. Whenever he agreed with something, he'd say, 'You betcha!'"

A deputy poured Lou a second cup of coffee as they worked. When the sheriff returned, Lou and Todd joined him in his vehicle for the ride to the Ada County Morgue.

As they pulled up to the morgue, the sheriff said, "This won't be pretty, men. You'll see him post-autopsy—that means a lot of sewing-up, the skull might be cut off, there may be sacks of organs. It won't be like seeing a corpse at a funeral home."

"I've experienced this in Detroit, so I'll be okay," Lou replied. "What about you, Todd?"

Todd had been quiet since they left the sheriff's office. Lou expected this meant that Todd was emotionally involved, with his mind totally on seeing his dead grandfather. But Todd showed no emotion, he simply nodded, a blank expression on his face.

"I called and asked them to have Harold's body on a slab. You'll have a better view than from peeking into a body bag. I also asked them to get a DNA sample, make a mold of his bite, and to take fingerprints."

"Thank you very much," Lou replied.

The three men walked into the morgue, removed their heavy coats, gloves, and boots, and waited a few minutes for the pathologist to join them. The waiting room was empty; it offered only a few magazines on a low table in front of a few chairs. Lou thought it ironic that one of the magazines was an old edition of Life and next to it was a copy of Better Homes and Gardens. Probably no visitor would notice the connection between the magazines and the building they were in. The magazines seem to beg depressed, sad people to pick them up, to get their minds off reality, in the form of a dead friend or relative to identify.

The office door opened and a man in a suit appeared. "Hello. I'm Doctor Alpert."

"Pleased to meet you, Dr. Albert," Lou said presenting his hand in greeting.

"Alpert, like Herb Alpert, the trumpet player," the doctor corrected Lou gently. "No relation." When he shook Todd's hand; Todd remained stoic. "I presume you're here to view the remains of Harold Moody. Follow me, please."

The three followed Dr. Alpert down a long hall with closed doors on both sides to a cluster of offices. The doctor finally stopped at a double door, opened one side, and turned on an overhead light. The four took places around a mound on the central table. Then Dr. Alpert removed the sheet, revealing the pale remains of an old man.

After a moment, Lou asked gently, "Is this your grandfather, Todd?" Todd looked at the dead man's face and replied in a soft voice, "This is my gramps." Tears began falling over Todd's pale face. Lou moved to support Todd, helping him into a chair in front of a desk in a corner of the room.

"You going to be okay, Todd?" Lou asked. Todd nodded, then rested his head on his folded arms on the desk. "Try to relax, and take some deep breaths," Lou suggested. "The doctor is getting you some water."

Lou returned to the body and the sheriff. "I never knew the man, so I don't know whether or not this is the Harry Moody I'm trying to find. But the DNA information, the fingerprints, and the dental bite-mold should provide some answers when I get home."

"You might find something in the cabin to identify him," the sheriff reminded Lou.

"Yes, that's true." Lou looked a long time at the face of the corpse, as he wanted to memorize any identifying features, any moles on the face, scars on visible parts of the body, strange-shaped earlobes. The doctor parted the lifeless beard, which by now had turned into a bristle-patch, so Lou could find any facial scars or marks. But there appeared to be no identifiable markings. Lou thought to himself, This guy looks like Harry, at least from the photos I've seen in Houghton Lake.

Lou glanced over at Todd, who was sobbing quietly. He put his hand on Todd's shoulder; he said nothing, for he simply wanted Todd to know he was not alone in his sadness. As Lou comforted Todd, it dawned on him that given Todd's habitual lying, the man before them probably was not Harry Moody of Houghton Lake.

❄✳❄✳❄

Four-wheel drive was essential to get from town to the cabin the "hermit," Harry Moody had called home; snow and ice did not deter the vehicle from the route to the hermit's cabin. The sheriff unlocked a padlock and pushed open the cabin door. Despite the daylight, the sheriff shone a powerful flashlight about the one-room cabin. There was no power, although a little sunlight shone through two small windows.

Todd elected to stay in the cruiser while Lou sifted through what appeared to be the accumulation of a packrat. He found wild animal skins, stacks of newspapers, books that belonged to the local library. Lou even looked at the walls, to see what the man had thought worthy of display. Nothing seemed out of place until he glanced above the head of the rustic bed. There, in a frame, was a copy of the Resorter obituary of Harry Moody of Houghton Lake.

"Is this odd, or what?" Lou asked the sheriff. "I need that framed obit." Sheriff Bingham nodded.

"What does this say to you, Sheriff?" Lou asked, wanting an objective and official opinion.

"Appears that somehow he got a copy of his own obituary from Michigan and put it in a frame. It could have been a reminder of his past life, or he may have considered it proof that he successfully fooled friends, relatives, and law enforcement."

"Very, very interesting," was all Lou could say. The men continued to look about the cabin, but they found nothing else of interest. It was all rather smelly, since varmints had moved in and made the place their home.

As Lou and the sheriff walked through snowbanks on their way to the car, Lou said, "I'll not say anything about this framed obit. Todd's had enough upset for the day."

"Agreed," the sheriff replied.

Back at the airport, Lou thanked the sheriff for his help and hospitality.

"Let me know how you solve your cold case, Lou. I have to admit, I'm quite curious."

"Certainly, Sheriff." They exchanged parting handshakes before Lou and Todd boarded the first of their three flights back to Michigan.

❄❄❄❄❄

Lou felt sure that the body on the slab in Idaho was Harry Moody, the center of his cold case—not because Todd said so, but because the framed obit made it logical. Otherwise, why would a hermit in Idaho have an obit from Michigan, framed no less, on the wall of his cabin? The flights to Michigan were uneventful and on time. Todd remained quiet all the way home.

As Lou drove to Grand Haven, he tried to account for Todd's behavior. Anything is possible, he thought. Todd could be telling either a lie or the truth. Todd could have helped Harry stage his murder and manage his escape from Houghton Lake. Todd could have sent him the obit when it appeared in the Resorter. Todd could actually be grieving the loss of his gramps. Or, Todd could be playing a complicated game. Everything was possible—or preposterous.

Carol was reading in bed when Lou parked his car in the garage, petted Samm, and removed his coat. He checked the mail and a few messages Carol had left on the kitchen table, then dragged his tired body to bed. It had been a 20-hour day, but one that might figure prominently in solving the case.

CHAPTER
SEVEN

The next morning Lou called Jack and asked to meet him at the Traverse Bay Pie Company on Apple Avenue in Muskegon. At around ten o'clock they went to work on coffee and bagels.

"Well, was the trip to Idaho worth the time, money, and energy?" Jack asked.

"Indeed. I'm pretty sure the Harold Moody of Idaho is our man. He had a framed obit of our Harry Moody hanging on a wall in his cabin. I figure someone in Houghton Lake sent it to him—and that someone is probably Todd Moody."

"Did Todd say the corpse was his grandfather?" Jack asked.

"Yes, he did, and he showed normal emotions of sadness."

"That means the man is not 'our' man, Lou. Haven't you learned to go with the opposite of what Todd says?"

"Well, yes and no. He's been honest in a few instances, which is what throws me off."

"You've taught me well. You've taught me to doubt the obvious, and I'm surprised you're not full of doubt."

"Why should I be in this instance? In doubt of what?" Lou asked.

"Well, here's one logical possibility. This hermit guy somehow finds the obit on our Harry and decides to assume his identity. He's on the run from something and needs to be somebody else. He works out how the man dressed, looked, and what he was known for. He simply takes the name and does what he can to look like him. There's no solid identity: no driver's license, taxes to pay, insurance, credit cards, wallet, or even a birth certificate. The man in Idaho becomes Michigan's dead Harry Moody, and who's to know or care?"

"You're good, Jack!" Lou exclaimed. "I taught you that?"

"You sure did. How many times have you lectured me about taking nothing for granted, doubting the obvious, getting facts to support the theory? Shoot! Now everything I hear, see, or experience I doubt, all because of you!"

"I'm sorry. Maybe Frankenstein just created a monster," Lou said with a chuckle. "You do have a point, Jack. What you say is possible, I suppose."

"Do you want another possible explanation?" Jack asked.

"No, I'm convinced, and I'm embarrassed for jumping to a fact-less conclusion," Lou replied. "You're right to put me in my place. As they say, 'the joke's on me.'"

"It's not often the student gets to set the teacher straight, so forgive me for enjoying it for a moment," Jack said with a grin.

"Go ahead and enjoy, my friend. However, all of this will be decided with forensics. We'll get 'our' Harry's dental records, a sample of DNA, some fingerprints, and BINGO! We'll have either have one Harry Moody, or two!"

"Now, you're talking like the Lou Searing I know."

❄❄❄❄❄

Lou called police Chief Warren Lincoln in Houghton Lake. "I just got back from Orchard, Idaho, where I viewed the remains of a local who went by the name of Harold Moody. I have some ideas I'd like to run by you."

"Sure. Anything I can do to help resolve Harry's case, I will."

"Do you have Harry's fingerprints?" Lou asked.

"Yes, we collected those during our investigation in 1985."

"How about something for a DNA analysis: a strand of hair, or a fingernail?"

"We didn't have that technology back then. But, I'll talk to the State Police Lab in Lansing to see what help they might be in giving us an ID."

"Any chance there are dental x-rays for Harry?" Lou asked.

"We had no body to compare them to, so we didn't obtain dental records. But, at the time Harry disappeared, there were only a couple of dentists in the area. They've been here forever, passing the practices from father to son. My guess is that, if Harry went to the dentist, whoever he visited here will still have his file."

"Good. The autopsy technician in Idaho gave me an impression of the man's bite, in hopes that we could match it to whatever we find here."

"I'm sure we can find one of those three. We have good fingerprints, so those alone might suffice. But my guess is we'll be able to get DNA, and maybe even the dental records. I'll get on it and let you know what I find."

"Thanks, Chief."

❄❄❄❄❄

Next, Lou called Bishop Photography in Houghton Lake. "This is Lou Searing. I'm investigating the disappearance of a man named Harry Moody in 1985."

"We've heard you were investigating, Mr. Searing," Carolyn Hitchcock, the receptionist replied. "If anybody can warm up this cold case, you can."

"Thank you. I understand that you've taken aerial photos of the Tip-Up Town Festival for many years."

"We've been doing it since 1956. Photography and the Bishop family are joined at the hip."

"I'd like to see your photos from the 1985 festival."

"That's easy. We have photos from each year. Shall I send you a set?"

"Overnight if possible. I'll foot the bill," Lou said.

"That's fine with us, but if you can pare it down to what you're looking for, it would be easier for us to sort out the relevant photos."

"I would like aerial shots of 1985's Tip-Up Town, any photo Harry Moody might be in, and any photos of men on snowmobiles. Obviously, I'm looking for photos of Harry, or anything that could give me information about Harry and his friends."

"Okay, that helps."

"Is it possible for you to have someone identify the people who own the shanties in your aerial shots?"

"I'll ask Pete Zylstra to do that. Nobody knows Tip-Up Town like Pete. Before I send you aerial shots of Tip-Up Town itself, I'll ask Pete to put names to the shanties."

"Great. I especially want to know which shanty belonged to Harry Moody."

"You'll have it all tomorrow. We'll Fed-Ex it to you. Is there anything else we can do?"

"That's it for now. Thank you!"

❄❄❄❄❄

Lou called Jack at home. "Can you go back to Houghton Lake tomorrow? I expect to stay overnight."

"Yes. I can postpone what's on the calendar."

"Fine, I'll pick you up around noon."

"Noon? Why are we leaving then?"

"I need to wait for an overnight delivery. Once I get that, we can go."

❄❄❄❄❄

Jack had been thinking about his visit with Craig in the shanty. The idea of killing Harry and putting him down the fishing hole was intriguing. He called Max Royster at the Resorter. "Hi Max, Jack Kelly here."

"Solved the case yet?" Max asked.

"Afraid not, but we're making progress. Lou and I will be in Houghton Lake late tomorrow afternoon, and knowing Lou, he has something up his sleeve that he needs to check out."

"What can I do for you now?"

"Is there a hardware store in town?"

"Yes, and we've a Home Depot as well."

"Home Depot wouldn't have been there back in 1985," Jack muttered. "What about a local store?" he asked aloud.

"It's been there for as long as I can remember. It's a very popular place—friendly employees, and every little gadget you could ever want or need."

"Is anyone employed there now who might have worked there twenty-five years ago?"

"Shorty Hendricks. He's worked there since he was in high school."

"Is he there now, or is he a 'snowbird?'"

"He's there unless he's sick, but Shorty never leaves town. In fact, if it weren't for television, he wouldn't know anyone lives south of M-55."

"Good. Could you let him know I'll be in town tomorrow? I'd like to talk with him later in the afternoon, or perhaps early the next day."

"Be glad to."

❆❅❆❅❆

While Jack was talking with Max, Lou put in a call to Tina Darling, a geometry teacher at Houghton Lake High School. "I'm looking for a math whiz to help with a case dating back to 1985. Can you recommend one of your top students?"

"We have several, actually. What is the nature of your inquiry?" Tina asked.

"I'll have an aerial photo of the Tip-Up Town Festival. When I designate a shanty in the photo, I'll need someone to tell me the exact spot on the lake or ice where it was located."

"I recommend Wendy Myers. She could do that easily, and I know she is interested in forensic science. She'll most likely pursue that major at Michigan State next fall."

"I'd like to meet with her tomorrow, sometime in the late afternoon," Lou stated.

"I just had an inspiration," Tina said. "Could you come to the geometry class and describe the case and what you'll ask Wendy to do? That will boost her self-esteem and give her something to toot her horn about."

"Sure, I can't divulge specifics, but I can sketch out the basics of the investigation. What time do you need me there?"

"Wendy's class begins at ten-fifteen, so you should be at the school around ten. You'll need to sign in at the office. They will page me, and I'll come get you."

"And if I can see Wendy late tomorrow afternoon, I would appreciate it."

"She has volleyball practice, but I'll ask her coach to release her to meet with you."

❄❄❄❄❄

JANUARY 30

It was snowing as Lou pulled into Jack's driveway. The local radio station predicted light snow throughout the day, with an accumulation of no more than two inches. The Weather Channel also predicted cold temperatures. That preview was nothing Lou couldn't handle, so the trip was a go. As they made their way to Houghton Lake, they discussed what Lou hoped to accomplish during the two-day visit.

When Lou's cell phone interrupted, he didn't recognize the number. He answered, "Hello. This is Lou Searing."

"Lou, this is Sergeant Steve Ellington, at the State Police Crime Lab."

"Oh, yes. I've been waiting to hear from you. What did you find?"

"Sorry to disappoint, but we couldn't get any DNA off the cap. Time and water did a job on it."

"Well, thanks for trying."

"You're welcome. Contact us again if you need our help."

"Will do." Lou put the phone back in his pocket and explained the call to Jack, who entered the results in his notebook.

As they neared Houghton Lake, Lou asked, "Tell me again: Why visit Shorty at the hardware store?"

"It's a theory, that's all," Jack replied. "I'd rather not explain it now. I don't mean to keep things from you, but I'd like to look into something myself. If my theory turns out to be a dud, I don't want to feel embarrassed. But, if I am on to something, we may find what I hear quite helpful."

"Fine with me."

❄❄❄❄❄

Lou met with Wendy Myers and Tina Darling at Coyles— a family restaurant—in late afternoon, after volleyball practice. Tourney time was approaching and the girls needed to practice for the demanding competition.

After Lou introduced himself and explained the purpose of the meeting, Wendy said, "Thank you for offering me dinner, but I'd rather eat at home with my family. It doesn't happen often. My brother's gone a lot, I have late practices, and my dad often comes home late from his business."

"That's fine, Wendy," Lou replied. "This shouldn't take too long."

Wendy said sincerely, "I'm very excited to actually meet you—and to help you. I just hope I have the knowledge and skills you need."

"Miss Darling assures me you do, that you can solve the math problem I'll give you."

"Okay, please state the problem. I'm ready."

Lou produced the set of aerial photos that the photographers had taken of Tip-Up Town in 1985 and laid one on the table for Wendy to study. "I will select several of these shanties, and I need you to figure their exact GPS locations on the ice as they were in 1985. Said another way, if a given fisherman dropped a bowling ball down the hole in the ice inside his shanty in 1985, all things being equal, where should I drop another bowling ball today to have it land beside the first on the lake bottom?"

"Okay, I think I can do that." Wendy turned to her teacher and said, "I'll need to blow up this photo, get latitude and longitude, and zero in on the exact point."

"Good thinking, Wendy. You'll need to find a GPS device." Wendy took a few notes, lost in thought.

"I'll be speaking to your class in the morning," Lou said, startling Wendy. "I'll explain what is public about the case, and maybe your classmates will have suggestions for you."

Wendy smiled. "I expect to have the answer to your question by the time you arrive."

"That would be great. Thanks so much."

"Mr. Searing, may I ask why you need these coordinates?" Wendy asked.

"I'd rather not say. If I do, I'm afraid my theory will spread through the community, and I could very well be wrong."

"I understand."

"I will say that if your work helps solve the case, I'll try to give you the details first. Is that fair?" Lou asked.

"That's great. Thank you very much."

❄❄❄❄❄

While Lou talked with Wendy and Tina, Jack sat down with Shorty in the break room at the hardware Store. Shorty, as his name implied, was short and bald, with Ben Franklin-like glasses resting on the tip of his nose.

"Tell me, Shorty, does the store keep purchase records from years past?"

"What we purchase to sell, or what people purchase from us?" Shorty asked.

"What people purchase from you," Jack replied.

"How far back?"

"1985."

"Oh, no, we wouldn't go back that far. That's a generation. Our tax man likes us to keep good records, but I'd say we get rid of them after ten years. Why are you asking?"

"If I mentioned a person, could you tell me what he or she purchased in 1985?"

"Nope, I can't help you."

❄❄❄❄❄

JANUARY 31

While Lou and Jack enjoyed their complimentary breakfasts at the motel, Lou unfolded the enlarged aerial image from 1985. "After talking to the geometry class at ten, I want to ask Pete Zylstra about people who owned shanties near Harry's. Maybe we'll get a clue or two."

"Sounds good," Jack responded between bites of French toast.

"Can you discuss your theory now, or are you still working on it?" Lou asked.

"It was a dud. I'm glad I didn't run it by you, and I'm not going back to it."

"Okay, leave me curious," Lou replied, a bit peeved to be left out.

"What can I do while you talk to the students?" Jack asked, finishing his orange juice.

"Take this dental impression from Idaho and try to find Harry's dentist. If you do, see if his dental x-rays match this bite," Lou said, handing Jack the dental mold of Idaho's Harry Moody.

"Okay. I can do that. Anything else?" Jack asked.

"Yes, see if you can talk to Estelle Moody. For some reason she hasn't been willing to see me. She's given one excuse after another. If she'll see you, try to find something in their home that would give us a shot at Harry's DNA."

"Like what?"

"Oh, a strand of hair on a jacket collar, or a favorite shirt. Be creative."

"It's been 25 years, Lou."

"That's only yesterday, Jack. The technology is amazing these days."

"Okay, I'm to go to the dentist, and then maybe to the Moody house. Consider it done."

❄✳❄✳❄

Lou enjoyed the class at Houghton Lake High School. The students paid close attention as Lou explained the problem he had presented to Wendy. While Wendy had not yet completed the assignment, she was on the right track. She needed to talk to the county surveyor before she gave Lou the answer to his question.

"Wendy, perhaps you could tell Mr. Searing and the class how you plan to find those answers," Miss Darling said.

"First of all, I need to magnify the 1985 aerial photo. I'll establish a scale and determine the distances from two on-shore points that are fixed and visible today. Then I'll determine an exact distance between two specific points like a city block, for instance. After that I can measure a distance from the two fixed points to a given shanty on the aerial photo. The next step is to consult a United States Geological Survey map of Houghton Lake—city and lake—for longitude and latitude grids. A protractor and the scale for distance will show where the two arcs intersect, which will give me the longitude and latitude of the shanty in question. Finally, Mr. Searing can use a GPS instrument. When he enters the latitude and longitude I've determined, the GPS will guide him to the exact spot on the lake where the shanty stood in 1985."

The class listened intently and when Wendy finished her explanation, they applauded. Lou was very impressed, though the explanation was a bit over his head. He would have time to go over this with Wendy to fully understand the process, but the results were what would count.

One student, who seemed serious, said, "Mr. Searing. I've been thinking about your problem, but I'd like to ask you: Who in their right mind would drop a bowling ball into Houghton Lake?" The rest of the class snickered. One shouted, "Analogy, analogy... all the world is an analogy!" The rest of the class applauded, and the questioner smiled, shook his head, and turned red as a beet.

❄❄❄❄❄

At the first dentist that Max had identified, the receptionist checked the records and reported that Harry Moody was never a patient. She suggested she save Jack time by calling the second dentist's office for him; that office did have dental records for a Harry Moody, and Jack was welcome to view them. Jack thanked the receptionist and followed her directions to the second office in hopes of locking up the case.

Jack introduced himself to Dr. Larry Cobb, the dentist who had treated Harry Moody 25 years before. Even though he had a full lineup of patients, Dr. Cobb took time to help. In comparing his own x-rays with Idaho Harry's bite mold, he wound up making two cases: the men being the same, or the two samples being from two different men. "A lot can happen to a man's mouth in 25 years, Jack. That's why I can't be absolutely certain the mold and my x-rays are from the same man. Look here. The two teeth on the back right side are a perfect match, but if you look at the incisors, these obviously give two different bites."

"So, you say we've a fifty-fifty chance we're looking at the same Harry Moody from Houghton Lake who went to Idaho. Right, Doctor?"

"If I had to testify in court, I could not say that the bite mold from the Idaho man is from the same Harry Moody this office treated."

"However, you're giving me your best professional opinion, and I appreciate it."

"Sorry I can't tell you what you want to hear, but I'm being honest with you."

"Thanks for your time, Dr. Cobb. We appreciate your help."

❄❄❄❄❄

After he left Dr. Cobb's office, Jack called and talked with Estelle Moody. Estelle had managed to hold off Lou and Jack, but then realized that sooner or later she would have to talk to one or both men. This time she reluctantly agreed to speak with Jack and invited him to her home.

Once Jack was comfortable on the sofa in the living room, Estelle began the conversation. "I imagine you want to see or take something that was Harry's. That's what I usually see on television when detectives are looking for someone. So, I have a few locks of Harry's hair to give you." She went into what was obviously her bedroom, opened a small drawer and took out an envelope containing several strands of hair.

"Thank you very much, Mrs. Moody," Jack said.

"You know, I haven't touched one item of Harry's clothing since they decided he had disappeared. I suppose I could take his stuff to Goodwill or the Salvation Army. But if I leave all his clothes where Harry left them, it helps me think he might just open the door and come in again."

"I understand," Jack replied sympathetically. "I appreciate your help."

"Do you think the man from Idaho is my husband?" Estelle Moody asked.

"We honestly don't know. We have DNA samples from both men now. If they match, it means that your husband has been in

Idaho for a long time. If they don't match, Harry could still walk through the door."

"I wish that would happen. He was a cantankerous old man, but I loved him. He was true to me, and he loved our daughter and his grandson. He was basically a good man."

"I'm sure he was."

"Sometimes I don't want to know what happened to him. But other times I want the truth so I can bring closure to this."

"I understand. Thanks again for your help. I should get these samples to a lab."

"You'll let me know, right?" Estelle asked.

"Most certainly, I will."

As Jack walked to the car, he had another thought. He turned around and went back to Mrs. Moody who had yet to go into her house. "Sorry to bother you again, but I have one more question."

"You're no bother, Mr. Kelly. Go ahead and ask."

"Did Harry keep any records of business transactions, and if he did, are they in this house?"

"I'm sure he did, because he needed all of that to pay taxes. I didn't make any change in his closet, and I didn't open his big roll-top desk. He also had a file drawer full of stuff that I haven't looked at. You're welcome to see it, if you wish."

"Thanks. I'll tell Mr. Searing what's here, and if he thinks it needs our attention, we'll contact you."

"Sure. You're welcome to go through all of it."

"I think that's all, but please don't be offended if I come back with another question."

"I'll be right here if you do." Estelle liked Jack and felt good about talking and helping out.

❄❄❄❄❄

When Lou and Jack met for lunch at the Big Boy Lou explained Wendy's mathematical solution to finding the exact location of any shanty in the 1985 aerial photo of Tip-Up Town, and Jack reported his findings at the dentist's office and at the Moody home.

"It feels like we're very close to something important," Lou said. "If the DNA matches, we'll know he wasn't murdered, but simply made his way to Idaho. If it doesn't match, our cold case is back on the front burner."

"And, if he was flushed down a fishing hole in a shanty, we could expect to find his clothes and bones on the bottom of Houghton Lake," Jack added.

"The question is, which shanty's fishing hole would he have been pushed through?" Lou asked.

"With Wendy pinpointing each shanty, all we need do is get a motorized auger, drill through the ice, and lower a camera or other device to show us what is under the 1985 shanty location. Then we'll know whether there's anything on the bottom."

As the two men paid for their lunch, Todd called Lou, asking to see him for a few minutes. Lou said he was sorry, he didn't have the time. Could Todd tell him what he wanted over the phone?

"Yes, I guess so."

"Well, then, please tell me now," Lou replied.

"I said that the man in Idaho was my grandfather, and now I want to explain the framed obituary that you found. Gramps always dreamed of going west and living in the mountains. He said Houghton Lake was nothing compared to the beauty of the Rocky Mountains. The fishing and hunting would be like going to heaven. He also said he was coming into a lot of money. He planned to leave, but he would stage it so people thought he died or was murdered. He got in touch with me after he settled out in Idaho and gave me a post office box where I could send him whatever I thought he should have. I sent him that obituary as proof he had successfully disappeared. As far as the folks in Houghton Lake were concerned, he was dead, and he was free to live his dream."

"Todd, stop for a minute," Lou interrupted. He then said in a stern voice, "If you're telling the truth, and quite frankly, I've learned not to believe a word you say, why on God's green earth did you ask me to spend time and money solving a case you knew didn't need solving? I don't like this Todd. I'm angry! I'm angry with you for making a mockery of my time and talent. Do you understand?"

"I'm sorry, Mr. Searing. I am truly sorry." Todd hung up.

❄❄❄❄❄

FEBRUARY 1

Lou and Jack had accomplished more than they'd hoped to during the trip, and they headed back to west Michigan feeling positive about their next steps in the investigation.

In submitting the strands of hair for DNA analysis, Chief Lincoln asked the State Police Crime Lab to put a 'rush' order on his request. The lab tech's unusual response was a rather terse question: "Why the rush, when the case is 25 years old?"

The Chief clarified, "Because Lou Searing is investigating it."

The tech sighed in resignation, "Okay. We'll get to it as soon as we can."

Ironically Lou and Jack were discussing the case on the phone. Lou stated the obvious. "DNA is the means to find out whether Harry escaped death in Houghton Lake."

"That's for sure," Jack replied. "Dental records were inconclusive. If the DNA samples don't match, we've more work to do. What do you expect from the results, Lou?"

"These are two different men."

"How can you be sure?" Jack asked.

"Todd told me the corpse was his grandfather, so I went with the opposite, which means it was not his gramps; dental records are inconclusive. Seems to me that if the two men were the same, we'd have a more encouraging report from the dentist."

"Just to play devil's advocate, I'm going to say they're the same man," Jack said.

"Your reasoning?" Lou asked.

"Todd's emotions in Idaho. If he were lying, there would have been no tears. But his reaction, which appears to have been grief, tells me he truly recognized the corpse as his gramps."

"What's the bet, Jack?"

"I'll buy your dinner at the first Knights of Columbus fish fry at St. Pat's next spring in Grand Haven."

"And if you're right," Lou countered, "I'll buy you pie and coffee at the Grand Traverse Bay Pie Company."

"Looks like we've got a bet!" Jack grinned.

❄✳❄✳❄

Lou turned on his computer and saw an e-mail message from Wendy: "Your exact locations are for the shanties belonging to Buck Brick, Harry Moody, and a third person that Mr. Zylstra couldn't identify. What follows are the latitudes and longitudes for each shanty. Enter these data into a GPS, follow the device's directions, and you can stand inside each shanty, figuratively speaking, in 1985."

CHAPTER
EIGHT

FEBRUARY 5TH

Over the next four days, nothing developed regarding the case; no phone calls, e-mails, surprises, or disappointments. Lou was outside with his trusty Lawn Boy snowblower clearing the most recent three inches, when Carol waved from the front door. When Lou shut down the blower, Carol called, "State Police Crime Lab on the phone for you."

Carol handed Lou his cell phone at the garage door.

"Lou Searing."

"The Houghton Lake police chief asked me to call you with the results of your DNA request for 'Harry' and 'Harold Moody.'"

"Well, the results will either close my case or set me back. And the DNA show?"

"They are two different men, Mr. Searing."

"That doesn't surprise me. It's what I figured you would tell me, but I needed to hear it officially."

"The two samples give us two different men, and no expert could draw any other conclusion. They're like comparing an apple to an orange."

"Thanks for calling, and please thank your supervisor for moving my request to the front burner. I know it's an old case, but I'm near to closing it, so I appreciate your making it a priority."

"You're welcome."

Lou put the phone in his pocket and returned to throwing snow from where Mother Nature had dumped it to where Lou Searing wanted it, out of the driveway.

❄ ❄ ❄ ❄ ❄

Lou called Jack with the DNA results, and then he called Mrs. Moody. As a courtesy, he also called Todd, who insisted the results were in error—a mistake had been made at some point. Todd believed that the items brought from Idaho or taken from Harry's home were not reliable. The police always got it wrong, he said over and over.

Last, Lou called Max Royster, who immediately asked if he could write the story for the Resorter. Lou didn't see any reason not to, so he gave his okay.

❄❄❄❄❄

Lou thought seriously about Todd's assertions. Maybe the hair sample from Harry's home was not his. To be sure, Jack asked Mrs. Moody to allow a crime-scene tech from the State Police Investigation Unit to visit her home to see if he could find any other samples. When Lou called the Michigan State Police Grayling Post, the commander agreed to send an officer. He thought it unlikely a CSI could find anything, given the 25-year time span, but he was sure his officer would do his best.

During his visit, CSI officer Billings examined a shower in the basement of the Moody home. "When was the last time this shower was used?" he asked Mrs. Moody.

"Oh my, that was Harry's shower. I didn't want him in my shower."

"Did anybody else ever use this shower?" the officer asked. "Has anyone used it since Harry's disappearance?

"Not that I know of. Harry might have washed the dog in there, but I doubt it."

Investigator Billings carefully collected some hair strands from around the drain. "Did Harry have a hairbrush or a nail file?" the CSI asked.

"Harry use a nail file?" Estelle Moody laughed. "That would be the day! I figure he had dirt under those nails from when he was a kid. I think I can find his hairbrush—he might have used it before a wedding or a funeral." Estelle led the investigator to the bedroom to search the dresser where an old hairbrush lay.

When CSI Billings finished his visit, he had hair from the shower drain and other strands from an old hair brush. Then he spied a cigarette butt in an ashtray behind a sofa. "Is that cigarette butt Harry's?"

"Yeah. You know, now I'm embarrassed. You'd think I'd clean this place up, but I guess since it was out of sight it didn't bother me, so I just left his things and his area alone."

❄❄❄❄❄

Jack was doing paperwork in his den when his phone rang.

"Am I disturbing you, Mr. Kelly? It's Shorty—from the hardware store."

"Not at all. Having a sale you want me to know about?" Jack said.

"No, but I've been thinking, and I had some flashbacks to 1985 or thereabouts."

"What were they? I'm curious."

"Well, I remember that back then, a guy came into the store, or it might have been two guys. I offered to help them, but they said they could find things on their own. I was working the cash register when they checked out. I remember it because what they purchased was unusual for wintertime. They bought four rowboat anchors, four or five rolls of duct tape, and several feet of rope—not twine or cord, but heavy rope. I remember kidding them about their purchases, it being winter and all, but they said they were getting a friend some joke gifts for a 50th birthday party, or something like that. In fact, now that I think about it, I had to go into the back room to get the anchors, because it was winter, and they weren't on the sales floor."

"Yes, I guess you would remember something strange like that. Who were the guys?"

"You know, that I don't remember. I've been trying to think, but I can't seem to draw up into my mind who they were. I recall I didn't recognize them, and I knew just about everyone who lived in the area. So they must have been out-of-towners."

"This is good info, Shorty. I'll tell Lou. He'll appreciate your call."

"Are you guys close to solving the mystery?"

"I wouldn't say 'close,' but we're on the right track, and we expect to solve it before long. Thanks again, Shorty."

Jack called Lou and relayed Shorty's story.

"Well, that's it as far as I'm concerned," Lou responded.

"What's it?" Jack asked.

"Harry was flushed down a large fishing hole in a shanty on Houghton Lake during the 1985 Tip-Up Town Festival. We'll apply Wendy's information to the shanties we want. Below one of them, I believe, will be bones and clothes, and anchors, and rope."

"Which shanty was he in when he went down?" Jack asked.

"It could have been his own. The killer could have broken in and surprised him. Or maybe he was lured to one of the other shanties and killed."

"Lou, I don't want to be a killjoy here, but all of this could have been a set-up to fool the authorities while Harry laughed all the way to Idaho."

"True, but we're getting close to putting this one away."

"I agree, but I'm not holding my breath."

FEBRUARY 6

Lou called Police Chief Lincoln and asked him to find someone with a motorized auger to drill holes in the ice. He also needed an underwater camera, and the best source was the State Police Crime Lab. The Crime Lab agreed to have a device in Houghton Lake by the end of the day, and a technician who knew how to operate it.

Once again, the trip to Houghton Lake began in steadily-falling temperatures, and snow was in the forecast. This could be a key day for Lou and Jack. If all of their planning paid off, today would be the day they discovered Harry's bones. Lou had called Wendy and her geometry teacher, Mrs. Darling, inviting them to join the trek onto the ice.

In Houghton Lake, Lou, two CSIs from the State Police Crime lab, Shorty, Max, and Wendy gathered for a snowmobile caravan to the sites where, 25 years ago, three shanties sat on the ice. Below one of them, if Lou's theory was correct, would be a body, the remains of Harry Moody.

The first place they stopped was the 1985 site of Harry's shanty. The auger dug through a foot of ice, providing a hole for the camera to be lowered. The camera was mounted on a pole that extended to twelve feet. A lamp attached to the camera provided the light needed to see what was below. Lou and the technician watched the small monitor as the camera was lowered into the hole, but all they saw was a mucky bottom with lots of weeds. They hoisted the camera and moved on.

The second hole was drilled where Buck Brick's shanty had been located. Again, they drilled a hole and lowered the camera, but the monitor showed nothing to indicate bones, clothing, or anchors.

Finally the third hole was drilled where an unknown owner's shanty had sat in 1985. While Lou and the technician thought they saw something, the image did not resemble bones, rope, anchor, or anything else that might be involved in killing a man.

Disappointed at not finding Harry's remains, the crew agreed that the experience at least had been entertaining. "Thank you all for coming. I haven't finished searching this lake," Lou asserted. "I'm fairly certain Harry's bones are under all this ice. We just haven't found the right spot."

Tina Darling, ever the geometry teacher, mentioned the possibility of disruptive movement of water, pointing out that— although they're fairly insignificant—underwater currents exist in Houghton Lake. "The Muskegon River flows to the west from the north end of the lake, and that constant motion causes some small movement," she explained. "Although you may be over where a body was dropped to the bottom of the lake, you must realize that over a quarter century, some water movement might result."

Lou thanked Tina for the caution. "I'll take that under advisement. Thanks for educating us."

❄❄❄❄❄

While Lou was out on the ice, Jack visited Estelle Moody to review Harry's business records from around the time of his disappearance. After a polite greeting, Estelle escorted Jack to the dining room, where Harry's invoices, letters, and financial records covered the table. Jack took his time going through the documents, for any item might be a clue. Four days before his disappearance Harry had noted in his journal:

> *"Provided a gold appraisal for Mr. ??? Didn't get his name.*
> *He planned to sell it for market value to a gold dealer in*
> *Lansing. Billed $50.00, paid in cash."*

There was nothing else of interest in the records, but Jack wrote down every word of the journal entry, for it was the first reference to the assertion that Harry expected to collect some easy money.

✳✳✳✳✳

"We need to postpone this investigation until we can dredge some of the bottom," Lou said.

"Maybe there's nothing down there that would solve this mystery," Sheriff Lincoln replied, a bit frustrated.

"You may be right, but my instincts tell me something we need is at the bottom of this lake, even under a layer of silt."

Lou's cell phone rang. He took the call.

"Mr. Searing?"

"Speaking."

"This is Sergeant Ellington of the State Police Forensic Laboratory. I have results of the second DNA analysis on the two Moodys."

"Oh, yes. I've been waiting to hear your findings."

"Our initial conclusion stands. There is no question that these are DNA samples from two different men."

"Thanks so much. Once again, please tell your supervisor that I appreciate his support in completing the analysis as soon as possible."

"I will, Mr. Searing. We're always pleased to help you."

Lou put the phone in his pocket. He got Sheriff Lincoln's attention and said, "There are two Moodys. Our Harry was not in Idaho."

"Well, we wanted the truth, and I guess we got it," Sheriff Lincoln replied.

"Yes, but I'm calling the investigation off till late spring or summer. Mother Nature is beating me up on this case, and she's a formidable foe. Harry has been missing for 25 years, so a few more months won't make any difference. No doubt we'll need an underwater team again, once the lake is thawed and warm. In the meantime, Jack and I will follow up any leads, but this case remains 'cold' for the time being."

On their way out of Houghton Lake, Lou and Jack stopped to inform Estelle Moody that the DNA test results indicated that her Harry was not the man who died in Idaho. They assured her they'd see her next summer, once it was warmer weather.

And, as the wind whipped the falling snow into drifts, Lou and Jack headed home.

CHAPTER
NINE

During the previous five months, Lou and Jack had considered Harry Moody's disappearance from every angle they could imagine. They concluded that Harry Moody was dead, and that his body rested either in Dead Stream Swamp, to the west of U.S. 27, or at the bottom of Houghton Lake. But even if they found Harry's bones, they weren't sure his death had been a murder.

"You know, I wouldn't be shocked if the murderer was Todd Moody," Lou said.

"Your reasoning has come full-circle, eh?" Jack replied.

"It started with him, and it might just end with him."

"But, Lou, why would a guy ask you to find a murderer if he killed Harry?" Jack asked. "Does he want to be caught? Does he simply want to challenge you? I don't get it."

"It's obvious that Todd Moody has major problems dealing with people," Lou replied. "If he did it, I don't know why he'd ask me to solve the case. But I also don't know why he lies to me."

"Assuming that Harry was murdered, I suppose his murderer could be anybody," Jack reminded Lou. "It might be Todd, or it could be somebody who owned a shanty on Houghton Lake. It could be his son, Junior. They had a bad relationship."

"True. Or, if we look into Harry's business, maybe it was someone whose estate he auctioned—someone who felt Harry didn't do right by him."

"Yes, but Harry's reputation was good when it came to his business dealings."

"Again, true," Lou agreed. "His business log showed that he appraised some gold near the time he disappeared."

"That's our only indication that he may have been coming into money. Maybe he wasn't quite as upright as people thought he was," Jack suggested.

"Let's say he learned about this gold from a customer and couldn't resist the appeal of it," Lou said. "All he needed to do was steal it."

"Who in the Houghton Lake area would own or have come into possession of gold?" Jack asked.

"We've covered his friends, his family, other ice fishermen, people who used his auction services."

"That's a good summary, Lou. But when all of this is said and done, it may just be Shorty's memory—two men buying summer goods in January—that seals the case."

❄✳❄✳❄

On a warm June 28, Lou contacted a local diving company, presented his request, and found their fee reasonable. Going to the bottom of an inland lake would be a piece of cake for these guys, since they usually looked for sunken boats deep in Lake Michigan. Lou spoke with both the owner and the divers who would carry out his request, and everyone involved understood what the target was and how best to look for it.

The summer sun reflected brightly off Houghton Lake's surface. The city was enjoying an early season of tourists and the return of summer residents to their cabins and homes in the area. As word traveled through the community that today might be the day they finally find Harry Moody, there was a festive atmosphere in local bars. People toasted Harry and placed bets on whether anything really was left of the man after 25 years.

"I'll bet he's still wearing his White Sox cap," one bar patron shouted, and laughter followed the image in people's minds.

"Bet the old man has lost a few pounds," another bellowed. "That's one way to lose a little weight!" Again, everyone raised bottles or steins of beer and drank to the mysterious, missing Harry Moody.

While some used the underwater excursion as an excuse to have a little fun at Harry's expense, Lou was very serious; this dive would either make or break his case. If Harry was not in the lake, Lou had no idea how to find him or learn what had happened to him.

Max was taking photos for the Resorter's next edition. He also collected quotes from Lou and the dive team. There was an air of excitement above the serious mood.

Jack could not be with Lou on the day of the dive because of a church responsibility, but Lou assembled others to observe the dive. Wendy, Max Royster, and Todd Moody would join him aboard the dive boat.

The divers, along with Captain Will Stoops, brought the *Kenny G* from Traverse City to Houghton Lake. Once all of the passengers were aboard, the boat was launched and a GPS instrument was programmed with longitude and latitude parameters. Slowly the *Kenny G* made its way to where, five months earlier, a camera looking for the remains of Harry Moody had registered an unidentified object.

The *Kenny G* dropped anchor, which served to steady it, giving the divers their opportunity to go below. After several minutes spent putting on wet suits and checking that the air tanks were full and working properly, the first diver, Josh Angel, fell backward into the water. A few seconds later, the second diver, Judy Sisler, followed. Using fins, they descended toward the bottom of the lake, directly under the spot that Wendy had determined was the location of the unknown owner's shanty.

The divers had directions to where Harry's shanty had been in 1985, as well as where Buck Brick's had stood. Swimming along the bottom, they were looking for the proverbial needle in a haystack, because the bottom was deep silt. Wherever Josh or Judy reached through the weeds, they found nothing solid in the muck.

Finding nothing underneath the first shanty's location, they moved to where Harry's shanty had stood. Now in deep weeds, the divers looked like golfers in tall grass as they searched for the elusive remains—bone, clothes, or rotted ropes. They circled and poked and prodded, trying not to stir up the black silt.

After several minutes of no luck, Josh felt a tap on his shoulder. He turned to see Judy motioning for him to follow her. She gestured to the silt, meaning she had found something. Digging, Josh felt the outlines of something solidly rectangular. He motioned to Judy that he was going up.

Josh surfaced and motioned to Lou and Captain Stoops to come to the rail. "Judy found what feels like a metal box with a handle on it. Drop me a long rope, and I'll tie it to the handle. When I jerk the rope, pull it up. I don't know how big this thing is, but we'll get it out, one way or another."

Lou asked Captain Stoops to note the exact position of their find. Whatever this box was, it appeared to be located directly below where Harry's ice fishing shanty had stood in 1985.

Josh, with rope in hand, sank into the lake and made his way to Judy, who hovered over the find. Josh tied the rope securely around the metal handle. Once he was sure the knot would hold, he tugged the rope, and those on board the *Kenny G* began pulling the box to the surface. Josh and Judy were first to see that the box was the size of a small suitcase. As the crew hauled it up from the bottom, the movement washed off a layer of silt that clung to the box, apparently there for years.

As the box neared the surface it became clear that its weight was more than one or two men could lift out of the water. Captain Stoops ordered the rope rigged to the boat's lift crane near the stern, and an iron hook attached to a heavy cable was threaded through the handle and around the box. Slowly the box emerged from the water and swung over the boat; several crewmen guided it as it settled onto the deck.

Max was taking photos as if the Titanic had appeared on Houghton Lake. He could picture the front page in his mind; he expected to sell more copies of the Resorter next week than ever in the history of the newspaper.

But what did the box hold? The passengers on board the *Kenny G* imagined everything from body parts to the treasure chest from Treasure Island.

For a while, the box just sat on the deck. It was quite heavy, requiring at least two strong men to move it. Lou wanted to wait until after Josh and Judy had climbed aboard to see what they had uncovered. As they waited anxiously, the onlookers felt a growing wave of anticipation. Finally Lou gave the signal, and a crewman used large cutters to snap the locks. As everyone watched, ready to look away if the box held Harry's remains, Lou slowly lifted the top.

A few gasps and a collective "WOW" muttered through the crowd as the onlookers caught sight of gold ingots, gold coins and opulent jewelry. The sight of so much gold certainly caught everyone off guard, and the group seemed stunned. The sun glinted off the yellow treasure, which had not tarnished during its 25 years under water. Only Lou was disappointed, in the sense that he'd hoped the box would somehow produce Harry, or a direct line to Harry. Gold had been mentioned in Harry's business records, but now it felt like Fort Knox had somehow appeared in Michigan.

The find only raised more questions in observers' minds: Who put the box there? How long ago? Who did it belong to? Why would anyone in his right mind leave a box full of gold in a lake in the middle of Michigan?

When Lou heard the phrase, "Who in their right mind..." he looked over at Todd to gauge his reaction. But Todd was leaning against the rail, obviously upset. Although Lou had felt obligated to invite Todd today, he didn't approach him. He knew he couldn't trust anything Todd said, and he wasn't in the mood for more lies. Lou had expected it to be a banner day, but all he'd found was a box of gold whose ownership was totally unknown.

There were two main questions that Lou couldn't shake: Was the coffer directly below Harry's shanty by coincidence? Or had the box been sunk deliberately from Harry's fishing hole in 1985?

Lou turned to Captain Stoops. "Can Josh and Judy go back down, or have they had it for the day?" Lou asked.

"We have time and plenty of air in the tanks. If you want them to go back down, they can."

"Great! Is there a metal detector on this ship that works underwater?"

"Yes."

"I'd like them to look for an anchor. I realize that there may be several anchors down there, but if they find one near here, it might be something I can use."

"We'll try to find one." The captain walked over to Josh and Judy, who were resting near the stern. "Mr. Searing would like you to go back down, to look for an anchor this time. Take the metal detector—it should pick up a signal from an anchor."

"Not to be greedy, but can we keep the next cache of gold we find?" Judy asked.

"That's what makes this job fun. We find a lot of junk, but that gold was an all-time best," Josh replied, giving Judy a high-five. The two were still giddy after their discovery.

The two divers put on their oxygen tanks and again splashed into Houghton Lake, scanning the area under Harry's 1985 shanty spot with the hand-held metal detector. They found minor signals, which were probably fishing lures. Josh also found a minnow pail, but didn't think Lou would be interested.

As Josh and Judy moved along the bottom to the point under the shanty belonging to the unknown owner, the metal detector indicated something substantial below the mud. Judy stirred the lake bottom and felt a metal bar, which she suspected was part of an anchor. She pulled at it, but there wasn't much give. In the meantime, Josh noticed that the metal detector was signaling another find. Judy joined him and found another anchor in the mud, this one with a rope tied to it. Judy signaled she was heading up.

When Judy broke the surface, she removed her mask and reported to Captain Stoops that they had found anchors and some rope. At this news, Lou felt excitement stirring for the first time. "We need those anchors and the rope." Judy grabbed the cable from the lift crane and disappeared beneath the surface of the lake.

Returning to Josh and the anchors, Judy clipped the cable to one anchor, then tugged on the cable to signal the captain to winch up the load. Judy and Josh knew they had likely discovered something significant, but full understanding of the find would have to wait until they were on deck.

The captain powered the crane to haul in the divers' latest find. Expecting to see just two anchors, Lou couldn't believe his eyes when, minutes later, a bundle of anchors and fabric strips emerged from the water. There were a total of four anchors roped together, with what was possibly denim fabric stuck to one; tattered ribbons of duct tape hung from the ropes. Last to surface were several bones tightly roped to one of the anchors.

"Don't touch anything," Lou shouted. "Don't contaminate any of this evidence."

Captain Stoops ordered the crane swung to the bow of the ship, away from where the metal box rested against the wheelhouse.

Lou turned to Wendy. "Note the GPS setting for this spot." Lou took a deep breath, then turned to Captain Stoops. "Once Josh and Judy are on board, I'd like to head back to shore."

Lou immediately called the Houghton Lake Police Chief, Lincoln, and asked that he request a State Police Investigation team be assigned to Houghton Lake and to the divers' ship. The team would need to catalogue the evidence, he explained, since it had been pulled out of Houghton Lake and had not been touched by anyone. After ending his call with the chief, Lou took a few minutes to thank everyone who had gone with him on this hunt.

Unknown to Lou, Max had summoned a television crew and called Shorty. Word of the finds spread like wildfire, and soon a gawking crowd formed at the pier, hoping to see what Lou had found—maybe even a skeleton. But, they were disappointed. Chief Lincoln carefully explained that they had found anchors, ropes, fabric and a couple of bones, but ID was impossible at this point. Contradictory to the Chief's statement, word buzzed through the town that Harry Moody's remains had been found. That "news" started a new round of rumors about who had put him at the bottom of the lake, and whether the killer was still walking around Houghton Lake.

The State Police CSI expert spent the rest of the day tagging and collecting evidence and taking notes. Lou was frustrated with the rumors because there was no direct evidence the bones were Harry Moody's. They could be from an animal that got tangled in fishing lines or from who-knew-what-else. But, a solution to Lou's case looked promising, because several items similar to those purchased from the hardware store in January 1985 were now accounted for. And if they weren't the same items, it would be a strange coincidence.

❄❄❄❄❄

After the *Kenny G* docked, Todd Moody had disappeared without a word to Lou. When Max asked for a comment as the ship reached shore, Todd shook his head and walked away.

Lou was willing to bet his reputation that he had found Harry Moody's resting place. He asked the state police to do a DNA analysis which he was certain would match that from the hair strands found in the Moody home. When he called Todd to tell him of his theory, there was no answer. He stopped at the Moody house to talk with Estelle, who appreciated Lou's work. Estelle maintained she had long ago accepted that Harry was dead, but at least now she knew Harry died in the lake he was so fond of.

Lou began his drive home into a sunset of pastels. He called Jack from his cell phone, telling him more than he needed to know, but Lou wanted to be thorough.

"Sounds like the one day I couldn't join you was the most productive of the lot," Jack muttered sheepishly.

"Yes, I wish you had been there. It was quite something, opening the box of gold and then watching as the anchors, rope, and bones came out of the water."

"So where does that leave us?" Jack asked.

"We can get DNA from the bone, which I think is Harry's. Then what happened to him will be obvious. Now we need to find out who put him down the hole."

"Whose shanty was located above where the anchors were found?" Jack asked.

"The unknown owner. But that isn't proof our unknown person was Harry's killer. Someone could have broken into that shanty and disposed of Harry's body."

"We still have work to do, Lou."

"Yes, we do. I also think the gold we found is a part of the story. My guess is that Harry and the gold are connected."

"Thanks for the update. Let me know when we get back to the case. I can't wait!"

"We're never off the case until it's solved, so we're at work right now."

✳✳✳✳✳

Lou arrived home in time for a late walk on the beach with Carol. It was a warm night and the moon was high. With his new hearing aids, Lou could hear the waves lapping the shore and the squeaky sounds his bare feet made as they pushed into and out of the sand.

At the water's edge, walking hand in hand, Lou turned his attention to Carol.

"How was your day?" he asked.

"No dull moments. I attended a planning meeting for this summer's Vacation Bible School, volunteered at the Ronald McDonald House, and then spent the afternoon visiting friends in the hospital. I finished the day with dinner at Sahara's—I do love their hummus."

"I always appreciate it when you go to those places when I'm out of town."

"I know you do," Carol grinned. "And, frankly, it's a relief not having to wonder if you're enjoying your kabob or your pita bread."

Lou paused and scanned the sky. "It's a beautiful night, peaceful, with a heaven full of stars," he said quietly.

"I missed you today, but I sense that you learned a lot," Carol said, squeezing Lou's hand. "I seem to have a sixth sense about you. Your invigorating days seem to give you an aura."

"Well, the aura should be bright tonight, because it was a landmark day."

"And Jack missed it," Carol said.

"Yes—volunteered at his church camp. Good man."

"He sure is. So, is the cold case warmer?" Carol asked.

"A bit, yes. I think we've found the body. Now all we have to find out is who did it. Oh, you should have seen the box of gold we pulled out of Houghton Lake! It was amazing. There were gold bars, coins, jewelry. It has to be worth millions!"

"Who does it belong to now?" Carol asked.

"Probably Fort Knox, in the end. Right now, I don't know, but I think it and Harry's death are related."

"Do you have any idea about the killer?"

"Yes. Harry did an appraisal on some gold shortly before he was killed. And I think the killer purchased what he needed for the murder from a hardware store in Houghton Lake. But who asked for an appraisal, and who did the shopping at the store, I still don't know."

"You'll figure it out. You always do," Carol said with pride.

They stopped at the large piece of driftwood where they often talked over matters of importance in their lives. This time they just sat, with Lou's arm around Carol. They were thankful for each other, for their children, and for their grandchildren— and for Millie and Samm. Life had been good to Lou and Carol Searing. Eventually they stood, shared a hug, and headed home.

Samm was asleep when Lou got home. Samm's desire to ride in her red wagon wasn't as strong as it once was. Lou stroked her golden fur and told her he loved her. Her tail wagged as if she understood. Maybe she did.

CHAPTER
TEN

Jack made it his goal to find the owner of the gold. If the gold was connected to Harry Moody's murder, why didn't the owner ever retrieve it? The gold was in a box at the bottom of the lake to hide it, Jack reasoned. Whoever put it there realized that nobody would look for it underwater; but again, why didn't the owner retrieve it? He surely didn't forget where he put it, Jack told himself.

Another scenario Jack considered was that Harry had stolen the gold, put it down his fishing hole, and then the owner killed him for stealing it. But the owner never knew what Harry had done with his or her gold. So, the burning question—the answer to which could solve the case—was, who had owned the gold?

Jack had asked to review the bank records for Harry Moody, but found nothing out of the ordinary. A review of the records around 1985 showed no large purchases of gold. Jack spent a considerable amount of time on the Internet, learning as much as he could about gold: where it is kept, how it is formed into bars and coins. He found the Fort Knox site most informative. After about four hours of reading and studying, Jack happened upon a web site article entitled, "How to make fake gold bars." Maybe the gold Lou found is fake, Jack thought in surprise.

Jack called Lou and asked the obvious. "I know that you're having the DNA checked, but did you ask that the gold be checked for authenticity?"

"I guess I assumed that would be done by the authorities," Lou replied.

"Who has the gold now?" Jack asked.

"I don't know," Lou replied.

"Excuse me while I pick up the phone, Lou. You said you don't know, right?"

"Yes. I don't know what the State Police did with it."

"Are you sure they took it?"

"No..."

"So, anyone on the ship could have taken some of it, and you wouldn't know? Was it inventoried while on the ship?"

"I don't know that, either."

"I don't believe what I'm hearing!" Jack said, stunned with this revelation.

"I'm sorry, partner. My attention was on the evidence, which I assumed was credible."

"Well, we need to know where the gold went, or where it is now. And then we need to find out if it's real or phony."

"Phony gold? Isn't gold gold?" Lou asked.

"I've been studying gold on the Internet and learning how to make fake gold bars. It's possible that what you found is not real."

"So what?" Lou asked. "We're trying to find Harry and who killed him. As far as I'm concerned, it doesn't matter whether the gold is real or not. We're not jewelers; we're investigators trying to find out why Harry Moody was killed."

"We need to know, Lou, because if it's fake, there will be no record of it. If it's real, perhaps we can trace it to an owner, or at least whoever had custody of it before it landed under Harry's shanty in 1985."

"That makes sense—I'll work on it. Good thinking, Jack."

Lou immediately called Chief Lincoln. "Chief, where is the gold that we found at the bottom of Houghton Lake?"

"You know, I don't know for sure."

"Really?" Lou replied, surprised at the answer.

"My mind was on the murder evidence pulled up with the anchors," Chief Lincoln admitted.

"So, you didn't take the box off the ship?" Lou asked.

"No. I guess I assumed the state police took it, along with the anchors and other items."

"I'll give them a call and let you know what they say."

After ending his call with Jack, Lou called the State Police Crime Investigation Unit. "Lou Searing here. I need to know what happened to the gold that was pulled out of Houghton Lake. Did your people take it as evidence?"

"I'll have to check on that Lou. Give me a minute and I'll find out."

Three or four minutes later Lou was told, "We took no gold from the ship. Our team presumed only the items pulled up with the second load were to be evidence. We don't know where the gold went."

Next, Lou called Captain Stoops of the dive ship. "Apparently we've lost a box full of gold. Is it still on your ship, or did you take it off for safekeeping?"

"It isn't on the ship," the Captain replied, "that's for sure. And no, we didn't off-load it for safekeeping."

"Did you see anyone leave the ship with it?"

"No, I didn't. I'll ask the team and call you back if they know anything."

Finally, Lou called Max. "Hi, Max. Do you have the gold from the dive ship?"

"What do you mean, do I have the gold? Of course not!"

"Well, we can't find it. The state police don't have it, nor the captain of the dive ship, nor the local police."

"Whoa, I don't think I can handle two big stories in one issue. Millions of dollars in gold may have been stolen?"

"Well, I don't know that yet. I just don't know where it is."

"I suppose you prefer I not run a story about missing gold until you confirm that it really is missing, right?" Max asked.

"Exactly. It couldn't have disappeared. I'll find it and let you know when I do."

"That would be a great follow-up story. I might be in line for the Pulitzer Prize!"

"Well don't book your flight to the award ceremony just yet," Lou said sarcastically.

Lou would check with Wendy and her teacher, as well as Todd, but he fully expected they would say they didn't have the gold, nor did they know who took it.

❄✳❄✳❄

In the late afternoon, Lou relaxed in his recliner. "Seinfeld" was on, and Lou always enjoyed the characters on this show. There were guaranteed laughs in each episode. His eyelids were heavy, so following the show, he put his head back for a short catnap. As he closed his eyes, his mind began to work: *Since the gold was directly under Harry's shanty, Harry must have put it down the fishing hole. But before he put it in the lake, he had to get it from someplace. Or the killer could have found Harry with the gold, killed him, and then dropped the gold under Harry's shanty. Then he disposed of Harry's body by wrapping it with duct tape, tying anchors to ankles and wrists and dropping him in from the unknown owner's shanty. If I'm right, the killer would have to be either the unknown owner or someone he paid to kill and dispose of Harry. But, if that were the case, why didn't this owner retrieve the gold after the murder?*

Lou didn't want to lose the thought, so he got up and jotted down a note.

The house phone rang. "I'll get it," Lou shouted to Carol.

"Lou, this is Pete Zylstra."

"Yes, Pete. How are you?"

"I'm fine. I wanted to tell you that I remembered who used to own the shanty near Harry's. His name was Skip Stone."

"Skip Stone? There sure were some odd names around there in 1985; Buck Brick, and now Skip Stone."

"I thought of it when I saw some kids skipping flat stones on the lake today."

"This is great! Thank you very much!"

"You're welcome. Hope you wrap this thing up fairly soon."

"We're getting closer, thanks to people like you and their sharp memories."

Lou hung up the phone, wrote "Skip Stone" in his notebook, then looked up Buck Brick's phone number.

"Lou Searing here, Buck."

"Got Harry solved yet? I heard you found something in the lake."

"No, I haven't solved it yet, but we're getting close. Do you know what happened to a guy named Skip Stone?"

"Yeah, he died a while back. I don't remember the year, but it's been ages."

"Would he have died around 1985?" Lou asked.

"I think he died before then."

"If he did, do you know who might have had his shanty in Tip-Up Town in 1985?

"My memory is getting a bit slow, but I did go to his estate sale. He had no family, so I think everything he owned went to auction."

"Was Harry the auctioneer for that estate sale?"

"Yes, as a matter of fact, I think he was."

Lou asked, "Do you know where Skip Stone died?"

"Sure, right here in Houghton Lake—he was a year-round resident. The Resorter should have the obit. You should look in the early 1980s."

"Okay, will do. Thanks, Buck."

Lou called Max, who agreed to search for the obituary and fax a copy to Lou. About an hour later, when the fax machine in Lou's office came to life, Lou walked upstairs and took a single page from the fax tray. He read:

> *Thomas "Skip" Stone died March 27, 1984, at his home in Houghton Lake after a long illness. Mr. Stone was preceded in death by his parents, John and Rita Stone of Erie, Pennsylvania, and leaves no survivors. Skip was born in Erie, and was a graduate of MIT, where he majored in metallurgy. Skip enjoyed gardening, photography, hunting,*

and fishing. A memorial service will be held at the Lugars Funeral Home at 10:00 a.m. Friday, March 29th.

Lou didn't miss the MIT major in metallurgy. This certainly could tie in with the gold, he thought.

If Harry handled an estate sale for Skip's executor, maybe the name of the person purchasing the shanty would appear in his business records. Rather than make the long trip to Houghton Lake, he called Estelle Moody and asked her to look for the records of Skip's sale shortly after March 27, 1984.

About a half-hour later, Estelle called back. "I found the estate sale. He didn't write down the word 'shanty'—he simply wrote 'fishing supplies and equipment.' The name next to this item is Wm. Nester. This Wm. Nester paid by check, and I found a photocopy of the cancelled check. The check is signed by William Nester, and the address is 1437 South 14th Avenue, South Bend, Indiana."

Lou carefully wrote down the address, thanked Estelle, and ended the call. Next he went to his computer and put in www. whitepages.com. When the site came up, he typed in "William Nester" and the address he had written. To find a phone number for William at that address seemed little short of a miracle after 25 years, but surprisingly, the name, address, and phone number came onto the screen.

"Oh, my lucky day!" Lou exclaimed. He called Jack and briefed him. "Want to go to South Bend tomorrow?"

"Yes—and do what? You're just going to go and knock on the door?"

"Sure. Why not?" Lou asked.

"He could be a killer. Aren't you opening yourself up to a dangerous situation?"

"Maybe. Are you coming?"

"What time do you want me in your driveway?"

"Let's get an early start, so how about seven o'clock?"

"Are you going to call first to make sure someone is home?" Jack asked. "That's a long way to go to find out our William is on vacation."

"Good idea. I'll call."

When Lou dialed the number from the web site, a gruff voice answered. "Nester's. What do you need?"

"Mr. William Nester?"

"Speaking."

"I'm Lou Searing, a private investigator from Grand Haven, Michigan. I'm looking into the disappearance of Harry Moody of Houghton Lake, Michigan, about twenty-five years ago. Might I come to South Bend and talk with you?"

"Fine with me. That's a long way to come for practically nothing; but sure, come on down. When will you be here?"

"How about tomorrow morning, about 9:30?"

"That's fine. I'll have the coffee hot."

"Thank you. My partner, Jack Kelly, will be with me."

"Fine, see you tomorrow."

JULY 2

At 9:25 the next morning, Lou knocked on William Nester's door. The day was hot, but rain showers were expected later. A man who appeared to be around sixty opened the door. "Mr. Searing and Mr. Kelly?"

"Yes. Thanks for agreeing to see us," Lou said, following Nester into the living room.

"Sit wherever you like. My wife is off with a friend for the day. You two want some coffee?"

"Thank you. We both like it black."

"Coming right up. You wouldn't mind if I threw a few sugar cookies on the tray, would you?"

"Fine with us," Lou replied.

Nester soon returned to the living room and served the coffee and cookies. He then sat in a recliner and said, "Okay, 'Murder in Tip-Up Town: A Cold Case'—is that the topic of this morning's conversation?"

"We're not certain it was murder, although we're fairly sure that it was," Lou replied.

"So, how do I figure into your investigation?" William asked.

"We've learned of a shanty that may have belonged to a Thomas 'Skip' Stone," Lou replied. "Then we found Harry Moody's business records that show you bought the shanty and other 'fishing equipment' in 1984."

"Yes, I did. My family has owned a cottage in Houghton Lake for many years. We'd spend our summers up there, and we really liked the area. One day I saw an ad for an estate sale. I looked into it and decided some things were of interest. So I went to the auction site, looked over the items, and decided to bid on the shanty and all of the man's fishing gear."

"Harry Moody was the auctioneer?" Jack asked.

"Yes. He was a rough-looking guy, beard, 'scruffy,' if I recall correctly. He had a few people working for him, which makes sense, because it was a big sale."

"So, you bought the shanty and the fishing equipment?" Lou asked.

"Yeah, I did. Good deal actually—only one or two bidders. I paid by check, and I hauled it away in my truck."

"So, Skip Stone's shanty was on the ice during the 1985 Tip-Up Town Festival?" Jack asked.

"Wait, there's more to the story. When I got home, I called to the wife to come and inspect the purchase. She stepped into the shanty, lifted the lid of the storage bench, and found this strange black box, about the size of a small suitcase. When she opened it, she found gold bars, coins, jewelry."

"I'll bet that was a surprise," Lou said.

"I couldn't believe my eyes. I'm a 'finders-keepers' type of guy, but my wife is a 'This needs to be returned!' type. So guess what? We returned it."

"Ouch, right?" Jack asked.

"Big time ouch!" Nester replied. "I called Moody and told him to stop over to the cottage because there was something we needed to discuss."

"He came alone?" Lou asked.

"No, he had a teen-aged boy with him—his grandson, I think. Anyway, I explained that we'd found this box full of gold under the seat in the shanty, and we wanted to be honest because we didn't think a box of gold came with the shanty."

"What was his reaction?" Jack asked, reaching for another cookie.

"For a few minutes he was tongue-tied—he didn't know what to say. Then he mumbled something like, 'A box of gold was not on my inventory.' I asked the logical question, 'Who owns this gold?' Was it me? After all, I'd purchased the shanty fair and square."

"Did Harry claim it?" Jack asked.

"Not at first. He said he would have to get with the executor of the estate and explain the situation. I understood that, but I told him I was going to call my lawyer, too, because I might have a legal claim on it. He understood."

"So, Harry took the gold?" Lou asked.

"No, we left it in the shanty. I thought it was safe to leave it there; nobody else knew about it, so who would steal it? The next morning I went out to check that the box was still there, and it was gone."

"Gone?" Jack asked.

"Poof! Gone! Now, you guys are the detectives, so you tell me who stole it?"

"My first guess is Harry," Lou said. "But you or your wife might have brought it into the house or buried it in the backyard so you could blame Harry for the theft."

Nester came half-way out of his chair. "Oh, no, don't go there, Mr. Searing! I told you what we did, and we are honest folks! Besides, I don't need a robbery charge on my record. But what would I do with bars of gold? It isn't like paper money, you can't use it to buy groceries. No, Harry must have taken it."

Lou and Jack remained silent, but they were both thinking, *Harry said he would be coming into some easy money.*

"Maybe the grandson stole it that night?" Jack asked.

"I thought about that, but I dismissed it, because the kid would be in big trouble when it came out. I guess I just didn't think a kid would do it. But, I suppose he could have."

"What happened next?" Lou asked.

"I called my lawyer who said he would get to work on our behalf. The gold never surfaced, so I couldn't claim it, and Harry maintained he never saw the gold after we talked. He thought his grandson might have told friends what he had seen and where. And, when word got around, someone took the box during the night. The following winter, I heard that Harry Moody may have been murdered. He'd disappeared off the face of the earth, just like the gold. I figured they had gone off together, and actually, I still believe that."

"Did you buy anchors, rope, and duct tape from a hardware store in Houghton Lake in January of 1985?" Lou asked.

"No, I did not. I wasn't even in Houghton Lake during that winter. We're basically summer people. I bought the shanty because I thought we might spend wintertime up there, but the reality was, I had trouble getting off work, and it's a long drive. I'd have spent more of the weekend driving than fishing, so we pretty much spend winters in South Bend."

"Did you lend someone your shanty that year?" Jack asked.

"Nobody asked, but I wouldn't be surprised if somebody just borrowed it for a season. It wouldn't have bothered me if I knew, but I never heard my shanty was taken without my permission."

"So, the only time you saw the gold was the afternoon you brought the shanty home from the estate sale?" Lou asked.

"That's right. And I sold the shanty about fifteen years ago. I'd never taken it onto the ice."

"Those cookies and the coffee were delicious. Thank you," Lou said, preparing to leave. "Any more questions, Jack?"

"No. Thanks for your time, Mr. Nester," Jack said.

Lou and Jack shook hands with William, who asked them to let him know when they solved Harry's case.

CHAPTER
ELEVEN

On the drive back to Grand Haven, conversation centered around the strange case of the Nester shanty.

"Well, Jack, do you think Harry stole the gold and put it through the ice in his shanty to get it out of sight?"

"If he did, he was the only one who knew where it was," Jack replied. "It explains why nobody came and got it."

"Right. So nobody else knew it was at the bottom of the lake," Lou said.

"I don't agree."

"You don't? Who else would have known?" Lou asked.

"I'll bet you five bucks that Todd knew."

"You're suggesting Todd helped Harry put the gold down the shanty fishing hole," Lou said.

"It could've happened."

"No. Todd wouldn't have waited 25 years to retrieve it," Lou theorized. "Again, nobody in his right mind leaves a fortune buried in a lake for 25 years."

"We're talking about Todd Moody, remember?"

"I don't care who it is or what condition he's in. If Todd knew where a fortune was, he would get hold of it inside of 25 years," Lou said with conviction.

"I agree that Todd must not have known it was down there," Jack admitted.

"Okay. So who would kill Harry?" Lou asked.

"Whoever stole the gold, because that person knew Harry knew the gold existed."

"So, who was it?" Lou asked again.

"I don't know," Jack replied. "Maybe somebody Todd or Harry told."

After a moment's pause, Lou said, "I'll play a card and suggest the killer was Junior Moody."

"That wouldn't shock me," Jack replied. "Let's take it a step further and say that Todd told his father about the gold. The two of them returned after dark, grabbed the box, and decided to put it down Gramps' fishing hole. Then they called Gramps out to the shanty, killed him, and down he went, too."

"There's only one glitch in your theory: the two men who bought anchors from Shorty," Lou said, not wanting to put a damper on Jack's idea. "Shorty said he didn't recognize them, and he would surely recognize Todd and his dad."

"That's true. We may be on the right track, but we need to stretch a bit more."

From Grand Haven, Jack continued his journey back to Muskegon, where Elaine was happy to see him. And, Lou and Carol pulled Samm in her wagon as they chased gulls along the Lake Michigan shore on a warm summer evening.

❄❄❄❄❄

Lou received a fax from the State Police Crime Lab. It was a lengthy report, much of it in medical jargon, but the part Lou was looking for was underlined. It read: "An analysis of DNA from the portion of left tibia bone shows a match to samples marked as those from Mr. Harold Moody of Houghton Lake."

Well, Lou thought, *Now we know for sure that Harry's final resting place was the bottom of Houghton Lake. Duct tape kept his clothes around him underwater, and four anchors held his body to the lake bottom to assure he would not rise to the surface. The water was not cold enough to preserve the body, and as it decayed, it no doubt was eaten by a variety of aquatic species. It makes no sense to retrieve more bones unless Mrs. Moody wants to pay for that service. We'll leave well enough alone.*

Lou had found Harry Moody—now he had to figure out who murdered him.

❄❄❄❄❄

Max Royster called Lou to ask if he could run a story about the missing gold.

"You don't need my permission to print anything, but I do appreciate your not wanting to jeopardize the investigation. The gold is still missing, so I see no harm in running the story. It's news, and who knows, maybe a reader saw something or heard something. Please ask your readers to contact me if they have information about the gold. You have my cell number."

"Okay, will do. I'll call Chief Lincoln as a courtesy before I run it."

"That's a good idea."

❄❄❄❄❄

The next edition of the Resorter led with the headline, Millions in Gold Missing. The story offered details of the box found in Houghton Lake including a photo of the opened box showing the bars, coins, and jewelry. Max's article ended with Lou Searing's request to call with any information about the missing evidence.

Within an hour of the paper's distribution in Houghton Lake, Lou got a call. "You're looking for the missing gold?"

"Yes. Who are you and what can you tell me?" Lou asked.

"I'm Karl Rooker. I was on the pier when you returned from your lake search. In the excitement, after the salvage boat was tied to the dock, a man approached me—he was maybe in his forties. He said he needed help moving a heavy box; he'd give me fifty bucks. I agreed to help. So, we went onto the boat and carried the box from the wheelhouse down the gangplank and over to a car in the lot. Sorry, I don't recall the kind of car. When we lifted the box into the trunk, I thought I was going to ruin my back for life, but we got the box in. I didn't know it was being stolen, honest. After all, it was broad daylight. He asked me to help, and I did. For all I knew, the man had a right to whatever was in the box."

"Did this person do or say anything besides asking for your help and paying you fifty dollars?"

"We were both moaning and groaning—that thing was heavy. I don't recall anything else being said. Of course, he said, 'Thanks' when he gave me the fifty."

"And you don't recall anything about the car?" Lou asked.

"Well, it was an American car. It wasn't a sports car or an SUV. I think it was a sedan, but I can't be certain. It was a typical American sedan—fairly new."

"Please give me your contact information so I can reach you if I have further questions."

"Will I get the one thousand dollars?" Karl asked.

Lou was puzzled. "I haven't read the article, nor do I know about a reward, so I don't understand," he said.

"The newspaper article said there would be a reward if the information leads to the recovery of the gold."

"I see. I have the time of your call and your name and you are the first person to contact me. If your information leads to discovering the gold, you'll get the reward."

"Any other questions?" Karl asked.

"Anything else about the man who asked for help, besides that he was in his forties? Beard? Hat? Fat? Thin?" Lou asked.

"He was white, not fat, nor exceptionally thin. He wore a baseball cap, but I don't know what was on it. He didn't have a beard or moustache. I don't think he was bald, but with the cap, I couldn't be sure."

"Did he limp or have a recognizable feature, such as a scar?"

"He didn't limp and I don't remember any scar. My attention was on trying to hold onto the box and then get it into the car's trunk. I looked at him when he asked me to help and again when he gave me the money, but I don't remember enough to pick him out of a lineup."

"When he approached you, did he come from the ship, or from behind, or from the side?" Lou asked.

"I was talking with a friend, and all of a sudden he was there, talking to me. I don't know where he came from."

"Okay, thanks," Lou said. "You've been very helpful."

"If I think of anything else I'll call you."

❄❄❄❄❄

A short time later, Lou received another call. A man's voice said, "I'm calling because of the newspaper article about the missing box of gold."

"Yes, what can you tell me?" Lou asked.

"It's not about the missing gold, but it's about the other things the diver found."

"Okay."

"When I read that the divers found anchors, duct tape, and rope, I flashed backed to many years ago, when a woman asked my buddy and me for help. She stopped us outside the hardware store and asked us to go in and purchase those items. She gave me enough money to cover the cost. She said she would feel foolish asking for them in the dead of winter, but she needed them for a gift. My buddy and I went in and got the items— it was no big deal. We walked out and took the items to her at her car. We gave her the change, and she gave us a tip for our trouble. The anchors were quite heavy."

"Can you describe the woman?" Lou asked.

"Normal-looking woman. It was a long time ago, but I'd say she was white, middle-aged, short brown hair, normal weight. There was nothing strange or odd about her that I recall."

"Do you remember anything about her car?" Lou asked.

"It was blue with gold trim, and it had a University of Michigan "Go Blue" bumper sticker on it. I remember, because my sister was going to Michigan State, and I knew about the rivalry. I said something like, 'You're a Wolverine fan, eh?' She responded, 'Love the hockey team, football team, baseball team. My son loves the Wolverines, too,' or something like that.

"Well, that's all I have for you. I suppose I'm not in line for the reward because this doesn't have anything to do with the missing gold."

"Your story is important nonetheless. May I please get your contact information, in case I need to talk with you again?" The caller provided his name and phone number.

✳✳✳✳✳

Jack called just as Lou ended the second call. "I've been studying gold, and I've contacted several people, and Lou, that gold must be fake. It has to be!"

"Why do you think so?"

"You simply can't own that much gold without its being traceable. Everyone thinks the gold is real, but it has to be phony. If we ever find it and have it appraised, we'll learn that it isn't worth much."

"I don't doubt you, Jack, but I don't understand why you're so sure it's phony."

"In 1933, the federal government mandated the collection of all gold. It was illegal for a U.S. citizen to own gold, and people were given other coin and currency in exchange for the gold they turned in. All of the gold collected is stored at Fort Knox in Kentucky. There is gold elsewhere in the world—it is traded daily. But that gold is all traceable. Trading now leaves a paper trail, and not much gold out there isn't accounted for. The FBI has no record of a missing 'box' of gold. Nor do any of the major gold brokers I contacted know of any missing gold."

"You've been busy," Lou said.

"Well, you know me: once I latch onto an assignment, I try to go all the way. I'm not certain the gold is phony, but I think there's a good chance the yellow stuff you saw on the deck of that ship is not gold. To borrow a phrase, 'It's fools' gold'."

"I hope we find the box so you can earn your prize for that prediction."

"It was hidden for 25 years; let's hope it's not gone for another twenty-five."

❅❆❅❆❅

Lou tried repeatedly to reach Todd, but each time, he got no answer. Todd was the only person on the dive boat that Lou hadn't talked with concerning the missing gold. Maybe Todd knew where it was—or maybe he took it himself.

Finally Lou called Jack. "I'm going back to Houghton Lake to find Todd, even if I can't believe a word he says. Can you go?"

"Sorry, Lou. I can't go tomorrow. I promised Elaine that I'd be here."

"That's fine. I only want to talk with Todd. I can't get him on the phone, so I'll need to see him in person."

"Let me know his latest lie. I'll have my cell with me."

Lou left early on July 3. It was a bright, clear summer day, just right for outside fun. The beach in Grand Haven would be full of people. The golf courses would have tee-times all day long. It would be a perfect summer day.

When Lou pulled into Houghton Lake two hours later, he called Todd one more time, but there was still no answer. So, he drove to Roscommon and pulled into Todd's driveway. Several newspapers were scattered on the concrete. If Todd had left, he'd failed to suspend his subscription.

Lou knocked on the front door, expecting no answer given the papers on the driveway. He knocked again, hoping Todd would open the door. Nothing.

Lou went around to the garage to see if the Hummer was there. The motor home was parked next to the garage, so Todd hadn't taken that wherever he went. Lou was surprised to find a small door, on the north side of the garage, open. He cautiously stepped into semi-darkness and flipped on the light switch. Directly in front of him, hanging from a rafter, was the still body of Todd Moody. His head tilted unnaturally to the right, from a noose around his neck; his body hung like a wet rag. On the floor under Todd's feet was the metal box of gold.

Lou quickly stepped out of the garage and called 911 on his cell phone. He also called Chief Lincoln to tell him what he had found. While waiting for the EMS unit to arrive, he went back into the garage. On one wall was an old license plate and a photograph of the University of Michigan hockey team—the Champions of the West. Lou instantly recalled the U of M conversation that allegedly took place between the woman at the hardware store and the two men that helped her with her purchase. That woman could have been Todd's mother.

The ambulance arrived, sirens blaring, and a Roscommon County sheriff's vehicle close behind. The sheriff and coroner would collect evidence to determine that Todd acted alone and was not murdered.

After two hours, the authorities had completed their work. The sheriff asked Chief Lincoln to inform Todd's mother of the suicide. He asked Lou if he wanted to come along.

"Yes," Lou replied. "I want to meet Todd's mother."

Lou could tell Sherri Moody suspected horrible news when she saw Chief Lincoln at her door. She invited both men inside, and then, anticipating what she was about to hear, she burst into tears, sitting back on the sofa.

Chief Lincoln broke the news with compassion, "I'm sorry, Mrs. Moody, to tell you that Todd is dead. We found him in his garage. He committed suicide." She continued to cry, holding her head in her hands.

"I was afraid something like this would happen," she sobbed. "I tried to get him help, but people wouldn't listen. He was a compulsive liar, but the local doctors didn't know what to do.

They recommended specialists, but those doctors practice in major hospitals in big cities and Todd refused to go."

Lou had a number of issues that needed clarification, but Sherri Moody was in no condition to discuss those concerns. However, to Lou's surprise, Sherri looked up, dried her eyes, looked directly at Lou, and said, "I've been expecting to see you for some time. You'll want to talk about Todd. I'll tell you what I know in hopes that you can bring closure to what happened twenty-five years ago."

"I do have questions, but this is not the right time to ask them," Lou replied.

"No, let's talk. I've waited twenty-five years to get this off of my chest. There's no sense prolonging the agony."

Chief Lincoln became an observer, partly to be sure that Lou's questioning did not violate Sherri's Miranda rights, and partly to hear what she had to say.

"Would you like a lawyer present?" Lou asked. "It might be a good idea, so that later there's no challenge to what you say."

"I guess that's a good idea." Sherri went to her phone book, then made a short call. "Attorney Janice Brown was in her office and will be here presently," Sherri said, returning to the sofa.

When Ms. Brown arrived, she and Sherri retired to the kitchen for almost ten minutes. When they returned to the living room, Ms. Brown nodded at Lou, who began.

"Last January, your son asked me to investigate Harry Moody's disappearance. I took on the case, not at all certain whether I could find any evidence to explain his disappearance. Over the last six months, I've interviewed several people and gathered evidence from Harry's home and from the bottom of Houghton Lake."

"You think my client has information about this case?" Attorney Brown asked.

"Yes, I do," Lou replied, with conviction.

"Proceed," she said, glancing at Sherri.

"In 1985, did you ask two men to purchase anchors, rope, and duct tape from a local hardware store?" Lou asked, getting right to the point.

Sherri Moody looked at her lawyer, who nodded as a signal to answer the question.

She looked back at Lou and quietly said, "Yes."

"What did you do with the items, once you had them?"

"I brought them home to my husband."

"For the record, that would be Harry Moody Jr., known as Junior, correct?" Lou asked.

"Yes."

"Do you know what Junior planned to do with the items you purchased?"

"He needed them to murder his father, Harry Moody."

Taking a few seconds to breathe deeply, Lou asked. "Did he act alone?"

Sherri's calm demeanor dissolved into tears. "No," Sherri said. The three waited until she pulled herself together. "It's a sad story, and it was a nightmare to go through."

"Yes, I imagine it was," Lou replied, sympathizing with Mrs. Moody. "May I continue?" Lou asked. Sherri nodded.

"I'll ask you outright: did Junior and your son, Todd, kill Harry Moody?"

"Yes. Junior had hated his father since the day he was born. According to Junior, he was abused by his father."

"Abused?" Lou asked.

"Yes, mostly verbal abuse. Junior told of experiences while he was growing up, when we were dating in high school, and after we were married. That's why I couldn't understand why he took the same road with our Todd. It seemed like Junior had inherited a trait of abuse. I could never understand how my husband could be so loving, so kind, and gentle one minute and then fly into a rage over the slightest incident. I'm sure this was the cause of Todd's compulsive lying. He grew up lying about everything to everyone, simply to survive."

"Did Todd have good experiences with his Gramps?"

"Gramps Moody was a good influence on Todd, in the sense that he felt compassion for the boy. But Todd's time with Gramps set him up for abuse, too. Whenever Junior heard his father had taken Todd hunting, for example, he'd hit Todd. Junior did not believe in harming animals, probably because he was harmed by his father. I'm no psychiatrist, but common sense tells me that's what happened."

"Tell me about the gold," Lou asked, turning a page in his notebook.

"I remember it very clearly. Todd came into the kitchen and said something like, 'Gramps and I saw a big box of gold this afternoon. It was in a shanty that belongs to Mr. Nester.' Apparently, Junior decided that he and Todd would go to the shanty in the middle of the night, take the gold, and then drop it down Harry's fishing hole. He made Todd swear he would never tell a soul about the theft or the burial of the gold. Todd went along with his dad's wishes. He only told me a few weeks ago."

"That explains how the gold got to the bottom of Houghton Lake, but how did Harry die?" Lou asked.

"Junior sent me to the hardware store for anchors, rope, and duct tape. He said not to go into the store in town because Shorty and the other workers might remember me buying those things. So, I saw these two men standing outside the store, and I asked them to get things for me. I gave them money to buy them, and they took them to my car. I remember one asked about my U of M car. He said he had a sister at MSU, and we talked a little about the rivalry."

"And you gave these purchased items to your husband?" Lou continued.

"Yes, of course. I don't recall when, for sure, but one night Junior came home acting upset, like he was nervous, or scared. He told me his father was dead."

"Did he give you any details?"

"He said that he and Todd had found Mr. Nester's shanty open on the ice. I guess somebody had 'borrowed' it for the season. Todd thought it was perfect for a burial at sea, and that's how Junior always referred to Harry's death."

"What made it 'perfect'?"

"Because the fishing hole was quite large. Apparently, some ice fishermen who like to spear fish cut a good-sized hole in the ice and then put the shanty over the hole. Anyway, Junior called his dad to meet him at the Nester shanty, which was near Harry's shanty."

"So, Harry went to Nester's shanty?"

"Yes. According to Todd, he knocked, then opened the door and came in. When he greeted Todd, Junior slipped some wire over Harry's head from behind him and pulled the ends till his father collapsed. They had put a piece of wood over the fishing hole to make a floor, because once Harry was dead, they could wind duct tape around his lower legs and his arms. Then they tied anchors to his wrists and ankles, took the cover off the hole in the ice, and pushed him through the hole. Todd said he slowly sank to the bottom, just as they'd planned."

"Then what happened?"

"Junior drove Gramps' snowmobile back to his house, where Todd met him in our car. Todd said it was the perfect crime, and nobody would ever know what happened. He was right—until you got involved."

"And, your son's lying?"

"As I said, that started when Todd was quite young and I know it was a way to survive. He felt he could control the world by making it conform to his version of how he thought the world should be. At least that is what one of Todd's school counselors told me."

"And yet he was able to graduate from high school, and Harvard, and hold a high-paying job with NASA."

"Yes, Todd was very intelligent," Sherri said with pride. "He earned considerable wealth, which allowed him to buy the home in Roscommon and his motor home and to live off the stock dividends from his portfolio."

"When he asked me to take on this cold case, a woman named Mary was with him. Who is she?"

"Mary has been a friend to Todd all his life. She's the one person who seems to understand him. She was important to Todd, because virtually no one else would have anything to do with him because they couldn't trust a word he said. But, Mary was somehow able to see through his lying and helped him get along."

"Does she know about the murder?"

"I don't think so. Todd told me that only the two of us know."

"Why didn't Todd somehow bring the gold up from the floor of the lake?" Lou asked.

"I truly think he believed that, once he brought the gold up, people would start talking about it, because you don't keep secrets in a small town. And, he didn't need the money. He believed that if the gold were ever discovered, it would inevitably lead to his dad and himself. He couldn't imagine being in prison, so, again wanting to control his world, he took his own life."

"But, why ask me to find out what had happened to Harry?" Lou asked.

"I don't know for sure, but I think he wanted the truth to come out. It's very hard to live a lie. I guess he needed closure in his own mind, but of course, we'll never know."

"Thank you for telling me this," Lou said sincerely. "Is there anything else you would like to say, something that hasn't come out in my questioning?"

"Well, you didn't ask me about the gold. Todd and Junior kept the box of gold here before taking it to the shanty and putting it down the fishing hole. They spent a couple of hours cataloging the gold, taking down serial numbers and whatever else was stamped on the coins and the bars. That list is in my study; I'll give it to you so you can check it against the gold you found in Todd's garage. And, by the way, you may think the gold isn't real, but it is. It belonged to a hermit, who hid it in a shanty near Dead Stream Swamp, on the other side of the four-lane.

"Todd told me that when the government demanded people turn in their gold for cash, this hermit never turned his in. Skip Stone bought the shanty after the hermit died of a heart attack. Every winter, Skip took his shanty onto Houghton lake, not knowing about the heavy metal box inside. Apparently he never took it out of the shanty—probably never found it."

"There's one more mystery to be solved. Can you explain how Harry's obituary wound up on a cabin wall in Idaho?"

For the first time, a sad smile came across Sherri's face. "I think I can. I'm not one hundred percent sure, but this is what I heard. That man lived in Lake City, west of here. He was sort of a loner. When Harry's obituary appeared in the paper, this man decided to take on Harry's identity, move west, and start a new life. It was nothing exciting, but he decided to become Harry way out there, and it worked for him until now. The man's real name was Ken McCue, and like Harry, he simply disappeared one day. Nobody missed him."

"Thank you, Mrs. Moody. I appreciate your observations. I'm sorry you lost your son. He certainly was a unique man. Do you think he knew when he was lying?" Lou asked.

"I'm his mother—I believe he knew what he was doing. But the only way he could survive was by controlling his world, no matter what public humiliation came with that effort."

Lou left Houghton Lake anxious to tell Jack all he had learned. Their cold case was no longer cold. In the warmth of a perfect Michigan summer day, the case was now part of the annals of Michigan's unique crimes.

EPILOGUE

Sherri Moody was arrested as an accessory after the fact in the murder of Harry Moody, as well as intimidation and withholding information in an investigation. The Roscommon County Prosecutor decided not to try her, given the time that had elapsed since the crime was committed. She was ordered to perform one hundred hours of community service. Sherri Moody gave all of Todd's property and belongings to Mary, the only person who had befriended Todd and cared about him.

Estelle Moody died within one month of learning what had happened to her husband. Knowing the truth seemed to break her heart.

Harry's friends used the funds Estelle left for her daughter, **Norah,** to build a two-unit apartment for her. They put the rest into a trust. The earnings paid for a live-in caregiver.

Doris Winston won the contest for the most fish caught during the 2010 festival.

Wendy Myers graduated with honors from Houghton Lake High School. She won a full scholarship to Michigan State University where she would study forensic science.

When **Shorty Hendricks** retired from the hardware store, the owner had a sign made in his honor. It read, "Hendricks Hardware." Hundreds came out for the unveiling.

The monetary reward went to 25-year-old **Karl Rooker,** who used the bulk of the money to buy computer games and to pay for physical therapy for the back muscles he pulled while carrying the box of gold to Todd's car. The rest he donated to a scholarship fund.

Former mayor **June Jacobs** told a Roscommon County Prosecutor that the person who had threatened her and other Council members was Sherri Moody. She hadn't told Lou because she feared the information would get out and she'd be targeted by remaining members of the Moody family.

Max Royster won no Pulitzer Prizes for his newspaper coverage of Murder in Tip-Up Town: A Cold Case, but he enjoyed working with Lou and Jack to solve the long-standing community mystery.

The gold was real, and court proceedings to determine the rightful owner continue. Lawyers representing William Nester, the executor of the Stone estate, the Norah Moody trust, and the Dive Company hold almost daily debates over who is the rightful owner of the gold.

Jack Kelly especially enjoyed helping find Harry Moody, and patiently awaits a call from Lou announcing another case.

When weather permits, **Lou** and **Carol Searing** still walk the shore of Lake Michigan hand in hand, thankful for each other and for all their blessings.

THE END

To order additional copies of this book,
or any others written by Richard L. Baldwin,
please go to buttonwoodpress.com

THE Musical
BALDWIN BOYS

Jackson Baldwin, third son of Scott and Patty Baldwin approached the school piano with confidence. The audience— parents of 4th grade students at Pine Ridge School in the Forest Hills School District near Grand Rapids, Michigan—waited respectfully as he took his place on the bench.

Jackson let his fingers dance over the keys as he flawlessly performed his selection. The audience expressed its pleasure and satisfaction with warm applause, smiles, and nods of approval.

Jackson is among eight grandchildren who may demonstrate a flair for music—a propensity, if not a genetic characteristic— that has appeared in the Baldwin family for centuries. Jackson's older brother, Nick, plays the piano, and his oldest brother, Ben plays guitar and cello. Younger Brother, Weston has yet to connect with a musical instrument but most likely will.

The gift of creating music will bring years of joy to the boys as well as all who will have the opportunity to listen to them.